A Castle for Rowena

Grotesqueries

Hayden Thorne

Published by Hayden Thorne, 2021.

A CASTLE FOR ROWENA

*

Copyright © 2021 Hayden Thorne
Cover art © Hayden Thorne

*

Written by Hayden Thorne

*

Also by Hayden Thorne

Arcana Europa
Guardian Angel
The Flowers of St. Aloysius
Hell-Knights
Children of Hyacinth
The Amaranth Maze
A Murder of Crows

Curiosities
Dollhouse
Automata

Dolores
Ambrose
Echoes in the Glass
A Dirge for St. Monica

Ghosts and Tea
The Ghosts of St. Grimald Priory
Agnes of Haywood Hall
A Most Unearthly Rival

The Haunted Inkwell
The House of Creeping Dolls
The Heart of Ameinias
Ada and the Singing Skull
The Dubious Commode

Grotesqueries
A Castle for Rowena
The Rusted Lily
Primavera
The House of Ash
Nightshade's Emporium
Voices in the Briars
The Perfect Rochester
Compline

Masks
Masks: The Original Trilogy
Curse of Arachnaman
Mimi Attacks!
Dr. Morbid's Castle of Blood
The Porcelain Carnival

Standalone
Renfred's Masquerade
Rose and Spindle
Gold in the Clouds
Helleville
Icarus in Flight
Arabesque

Banshee
Wollstone
The Glass Minstrel
Henning
The Twilight Gods
The Book of Lost Princes
The Winter Garden and Other Stories
Desmond and Garrick
The Cecilian Blue-Collar Chronicles

Watch for more at https://www.haydenthorne.com.

Chapter 1

"You haven't touched your food, love."

I blinked and glanced up, my face warming. The look being leveled at me from across the table was one of worry, and I nodded. I obediently picked my way through my dinner, the roasted meat and boiled vegetables barely leaving a mark either on my tongue or my stomach though I persisted.

Gray eyes normally placid and somber were now shadowed with badly suppressed anxiety on my account.

"I'm eating, see?" I gave my plate a light push as if he couldn't see it at all. "I'll be all right, I swear. I'm just tired."

"Edgar, you don't have to do this. It's been two years already."

"I—I know, darling. I know. But—a last visit. That's all. I can't—I'll carry on after this. We'll carry on, yes?" I braved a smile though my spirits withered a little under Cyrille's fixed gaze. "We'll be in France tomorrow, anyway, and we'll never come back."

That drew out a slightly relieved smile from him even if the worry clouding his eyes continued to shadow them. He understood what remained unsaid. The dreams—oftentimes nightmares—lured me back to Bridewater House.

"Took us long enough," he replied. Then he looked around us, shifted a little on his seat, and touched my hand under the table. He still had to strain a little to reach me, but he did it, anyway. "I promise you, Edgar, leaving England will be for the best."

"No more nightmares?"

"No more nightmares."

He blessed me with that roguish smile I loved, and I learned to answer back with a smile of my own (though decidedly much less roguish). I quickly curled my fingers around his and sought reassurance with a timid squeeze. He answered with a firmer and more decisive one, holding me a spell longer before releasing my hand.

I finished my dinner in silence while Cyrille savored his wine. He'd been done with his own meal several minutes before, of course, but then again, we'd always been polar opposites at the table. One might laugh at the thought that a Frenchman would eat hastily and without much thought while an Englishman would display proper care and idle enjoyment. A gross exaggeration, perhaps, but one couldn't help the joke in his head, especially one in my muddled and anxious state.

We followed dinner with a quick wash upstairs in our shared room. An altogether awkward business given how small and cramped our space was, but it did work quite beautifully to our advantage when the hour was right. Bundled up for a walk along the moonlit road, we soon headed out.

It was around a mile-long walk in one direction from our inn outside Bracklewhyte, but we'd done this for two years now that we no longer felt the distance—two years and two visits for each year, the dates having been chosen at random all from my end. And Cyrille, bless him, had taken full advantage of every trip to find new commissions for his art, an endeavor that yielded very good results. He was never in want of work, and his patrons were pleased.

With the patience of all the saints in history, Cyrille kept his place at my side on these trips and had grown used to my nervous requests. He'd even gotten very skilled in calming me down. In fact, we often lingered on the road to Bridewater House at his gentle insistence, pausing now and then to talk intimately or to kiss. We'd grown awfully confident in these late night excursions.

The night was our friend, the shadows our loyal guardians. The moon sometimes hid, but we'd been fortunate enough to enjoy her bounty almost all of the time. I prefer to think she blessed us with silver whenever she espied us on the road, offering comfort and guidance to her hidden children, allowing us the freedom and movement the sun would always deny.

Tonight was different in a way. Tonight was the night I said goodbye to my past and the ghosts that would forever haunt it. I would set eyes on Bridewater House for one last time, see my suspicions confirmed despite the fact they'd been confirmed for the past couple of years already, and this trip wouldn't matter at all. Nothing would change; I expected such a thing. Two years until now, two years hence, and perhaps several decades well after until Nature completely overcame the dreary old ruins—things would carry on within those walls, completely untouched by the world.

The road itself was so isolated and forgotten, it was a wonder it existed still, not at all overrun by wild things creeping out from the sparse wood around us. What a sorry destiny for a road that had once been used so frequently, tying forgotten towns and villages in the distant past. A catastrophic flood had washed away the old bridge linking a couple of isolated towns to more bustling destinations, and it was never rebuilt. The road now had a reputation of being haunted as well, and nothing keeps superstitious villagers from a long and lonely path like restless spirits seeking company during one's walk.

Cyrille and I simply held hands for the remaining quarter-mile, our hushed conversation fading into the night air. We eventually rounded a curve and immediately spotted the narrow drive branching off from the road to guide us to Bridewater House. Without another word exchanged, we stepped onto it and followed its grim progress through the scattered trees, the overgrown grass and snaking briars thickening impossibly the closer we got to the house.

What had once been a grand structure rivaling elegant châteaux was now a sprawling corpse of stone, timber, and glass. Abandoned and forgotten for years, Bridewater House was at the mercy of Nature, and it took every ounce of imagination I had to superimpose life, light, and activity on the bleak and oppressive ruins before me.

No, wait—yes, yes, there it was.

There *she* was.

"Cyrille," I breathed, my grip on his hand tightening reflexively as my gaze fell on the dim yellow light that could barely pierce the dirt-caked glass of an upper-floor window. "There! There!"

"Dear God," he whispered back. "Why does she insist? It's been so long, Edgar."

"I know. I know." I swallowed and shook my head in disbelief. "I can't help her. I don't think anyone can."

"Darling, she's beyond help, let alone hope. Even in life, you said, and now? More so now—nothing's stopping her."

"Death certainly doesn't, but this is her wish, isn't it? She said so before."

We fell silent again as we watched the feeble light appear to flicker behind the broken and dirt-caked window, and I could picture a single lamp being carried around from room to room. Protective, vigilant, making good a promise made to a dying mistress—a loyal and fiercely devoted servant who never shirked her duties and who took her responsibilities as her mistress's staunchest defender to heart.

And to impossible lengths, it looked like.

The night was clear and mild, but a chill rippled up and down my body, making me shiver and inch closer to Cyrille. Around us an awful silence descended, and none of the usual nocturnal sounds could be heard. There was a heaviness, a thickness to the auditory void we now found ourselves in. It certainly seemed as though Mrs. Quigg manipulated our surroundings to draw even more attention to herself as she carried on with her duties.

I often wondered if she walked from room to room every night since she breathed her last. If, for instance, her spectral lamp lit her way even when I wasn't there to bear witness to her promise. Or did she make herself seen only at times like this, when she knew she had an audience? This was the purpose behind my choosing random days of each year of my return to Bridewater House. I wanted to see for myself—to confirm my suspicions of Mrs. Quigg's nocturnal vigilance not at all ceasing throughout the year.

"Edgar, let's go. We shouldn't linger. Besides, your father's waiting for you, and heaven knows what sort of mischief that dear old gentleman can get into when you're not around."

Cyrille's reminder of Papa had a hint of gentle humor in it, but in the presence of the dead, my spirits refused to be lifted. How the deceased could have so much power over me, I didn't understand. They did, however, and it felt like being pulled deeper and deeper into cold, murky waters.

"Edgar? Darling, look at me."

"All right. I—all right." I sighed and looked up at him, my chest easing its strained tightness at the sight of the one person who made life worth something more. My constant, my future—my un-husband, I called him, a playful term of endearment he'd also taken up in reference to me. "All this would have been mine, you know. I mean, it is—but it never will be."

I'd turned twenty-three that year. Rowena's fortune had been legally mine for two years. Even Bridewater House though I'd turned my back on the property for very good reason.

Cyrille nodded, a wry little smile lighting his face as he regarded me. "Do you regret leaving when you did? Giving all of this up?"

"No. Never. In truth, I doubt if I'd have been able to manage it—owning all of this and living in it, I mean. The house, everything that came with it? No, I don't think all of this would have been fully mine to begin with. There's too much of her in it, and I just can't—she wouldn't have let her castle go so easily even after death, I think. Clearly, Mrs. Quigg agrees with me."

I looked back at the dark windows and the feeble light that had now moved to another room. Mrs. Quigg had found the previous room to her satisfaction, I suppose.

"There's too much of Rowena in this place. It's always been hers and hers alone." I paused and nodded at the upper window and the phantom light within. "Mrs. Quigg's making sure of it."

Cyrille gave my hand a light tug, and I turned away from Bridewater House for the last time as he guided me away. Hand-in-hand we arrived there, and hand-in-hand we left. I suppose we made for a defiant picture of life and hope against a crumbling ruin of past tragedies brought about by the human heart opening itself to its shadow half.

Indeed, we seemed to be the only ones alive in that neglected and overgrown land and its surrounding woodland. Despite the distance we were placing between ourselves and the corpse of the old house, the thick silence pervaded, and I could swear I felt eyes fixed upon us as we walked away. Perhaps Mrs. Quigg watched us leave her beloved kingdom. Perhaps she knew this would be the last time she'd be seeing me.

How far can the dead see, anyway? How much do they know about the future?

The awful silence broke the moment we stepped out of the drive and were once again back on the forgotten road, the moon offering comfort in her own mute and magical way. The road seemed brighter then, but I suppose one can't help but think that after being surrounded by nothing but shadows that seemed to mock her gentle efforts.

I couldn't rightly say how I felt that time. As with dinner, my last goodbye to Bridewater House didn't seem real, and a dullness and flatness pressed down on me and made me silent and distracted even as I prepared for bed on our return to the inn.

That night I dreamt I stood before that dreadful portrait on the wall behind the grand staircase again, gazing up at its expansive canvas with wide-eyed dread. Time dragged most excruciatingly as I was forced to wait, unable to move a muscle because the woman staring back at me in paint and careful brushstrokes willed me in place.

Unearthly pale blue eyes held me fast, the full and gracefully curved mouth slowly, slowly widened in a broadening smile, and red lips opened with a gentle sigh.

Come here. Let me see you. How you've grown! Such a beautiful boy!

Then she moved, her limbs slow and heavy as though she were moving through water. My terrified mind urged me to run, but I couldn't, and she refused me with her fixed, unfocused eyes and her ghastly rictus on a dead face. She reached out, stretching her arms past the canvas and frame as she leaned forward and stepped out. Her gown trailed behind, discolored and tattered and smelling of earth and moldering coffins.

My baby boy—let me hold you. Oh, my darling, how I missed you so. Stay with me this time.

She fell upon me and pulled me close till I felt as though I were being pulled down into the grave with her, and I tore myself out of my dream with an agonized cry that Cyrille managed to bury against his chest. He held me for a time, hushing my ragged, gasping breaths and terrified whimpers while I clung to him in our cramped bed.

It had become a ritual for us whenever we visited Bridewater House. The nightmare came first, followed by gentle touches and kisses. Then my nightshirt would be pushed up to my chest, Cyrille's thick length buried in me from behind, his hand pressed against my slack mouth to muffle my cries. Terror and dismay would release in a burst of physical pleasure that drained me nearly dry, and I'd drift back to sleep cradled in my un-husband's arms.

It would take me longer than before to recover from the dream—from the ghastly but necessary reminder that Rowena would have never allowed me to be the master of Bridewater House despite my legal claim to it. Despite her generosity in acknowledging me as her heir. Bridewater House had always been—and forever would be—hers.

Chapter 2

I don't remember my mother at all, but people had been very good in telling me when I grew older. They'd been all rather too eager, in fact, when I took the trouble of carefully digging. She was the fifth and youngest child born to a farmer and a seamstress. She was unnaturally beautiful—standing out from her brothers and sisters like a perfectly sculpted angel though also lacking in sense and restraint.

She was adored by rustic fellows and bore the brunt of jealous whispers among her peers. As far as I now know, she welcomed the attention and even encouraged it, toying with boys' hearts until she ultimately lost her gamble. She was raped by a baronet's drunkard son at sixteen, and I was the result of his treachery.

It had been said that my mother's refusal to toss me into a foundling home led her to being troubled day and night by her own family. She was called a whore. A dirty slut who'd bare her breasts and spread her legs for a flattering word or two. By all accounts she'd borne everything with her head held high in open defiance. Silent and proud, a tragic beauty till the end.

I was only a year old when a neighboring farmer discovered her hanging from a dead oak in the sparse wood near their cottage. And there I lay on a tattered sack, quite swaddled against the cool evening breeze, howling piteously while she lightly swayed a few feet away. To this day, I don't know why she brought me there and left me alone and exposed. Perhaps that had been her plan all along—to die and to take me with her somehow.

According to gossips, the farmer who found us had suggested that perhaps she'd changed her mind about me and had hoped for a rescuer to be drawn to my ragged cries. Who knew her mind then, anyway? She was seventeen then, still quite a child, rejected by her family and horribly abused by a man who had everything in the world but a soul. If she went about her plans of murder and suicide haphazardly, it shouldn't surprise anyone.

I was then taken to an orphanage, and there I stayed for a little over four years, content to be invisible whenever the occasional couple appeared for a child to take home. Not that it was troublesome to inch away from the crowd of underfed, ragged, hopeful children. There were simply too many of us and not enough childless couples to go around. Somehow I managed to elude every opportunity of presenting myself to a pair until I turned five.

A gentleman recently widowed—both wife and baby lost in childbirth a year before—appeared, determined to shake off his depression with a less fortunate child whom he could raise as his own. I'd been unwell and as such was too slow to plan an escape, and the grieving gentleman caught sight of me faltering in my steps as I tried to break out into a run away from the uniformed children currently lost in energetic play. The dreary courtyard serving as our playground was a little crowded, but I suppose I stood out in the worst way possible.

The widower—a Mr. Theodore Cushing from the small town of Bracklewhyte—broke away from the somber group of teachers and nurses and caught me just as a faintness overcame my feverish brain, and I stumbled to the ground.

"There, there—you'll be all right, young man. You shouldn't be out here exerting yourself when you're clearly not feeling well. Ah—your skin's too hot. Nurse! Nurse! This child has a fever!" he cried as he bore me up in his arms, shivering and wracked with miserable sobs.

I truly couldn't remember much of the hours and days that followed.

Suffice it to say Mr. Cushing, his heart touched, had applied to adopt me when the moment came, and I was declared quite recovered from my illness. I honestly don't know why he'd taken to me so quickly given my wretched state of health and shrunken appearance. Years after, I'd teased him about it, and he'd only smile fondly, a parent's love alit in his eyes, and reply with a gentle stroking of my hair and a kiss on my forehead.

My father wasn't a man of many words. Even after my adoption, he showered me with such doting attention and unrestrained love far more than expressed his affection for me in clear words. Not that I needed any proof of our close bond through the years because he compensated for his reticence with action. And that had been sufficient—more than sufficient—for me.

So for several years after it was only the two of us forging a deep—and dare I say unbreakable—bond as a family with dear Mrs. Murray being her big-hearted and generous self as she divided her precious time between looking after a tiny motherless household and her own. Papa hired her for day help when he brought me home for the first time, and she'd become my surrogate mother in so many ways despite her love for Papa being nothing more than that of a loyal and tender-hearted housekeeper.

Papa owned a very small and modest establishment—a tailor's shop that served mostly working gentlemen on a limited budget. He'd inherited the business from his father and had shown much promise in dressing clerks, other shopkeepers, academics, and other gentlemen who wished to appear as respectable and deserving of the public's attention and patronage.

"The wealthy—those generously inclined, anyway—often leave charity houses a collection of castoffs, Edgar," he said one day as I toddled after him in his shop in wide-eyed amazement. "I buy the excess quite cheaply and turn them into proper and respectable suits for gentlemen of limited means who work as hard as I do."

A piece of bread nearly crushed in my tiny hand as I pointed and spouted silly questions about jackets, waistcoats, patterns, and so on, I listened to him as he tried to explain what he did for a living, my seven-year-old brain barely making heads or tails of anything. Everything around me, I thought, looked positively marvelous and magical.

Papa sat down on one of the old and rickety chairs littering his shop and set me down on his lap. "See, not everyone can afford a good suit," he carried on, gently holding me against his chest while I gnawed away at the bread. "And there are far more bankers and clerks and schoolmasters and butchers than there are lords and baronets and so on. So I let, say, a bookseller choose something from my racks, and I take proper measurements and then turn his choice into something uniquely his."

"The clothes fit him right good, Pa?"

"By the time I'm done with them, yes. Perfectly. I also add a few touches here and there—maybe a spot of color to cheer up a somber waistcoat—anything that would make the bookseller stand out and be as memorable to look at as his books."

I pondered things a bit. "And he'll also be cheerful like his waistcoat?"

"Indeed! Why, colors affect mood, Edgar, though it's customary for gentlemen to stick to black and gray as a way of showing the world how dignified and respectable they are. The lack of color makes one think of restraint and a sensible turn of mind, both of which are qualities we learn to approve of."

I remember noting a hint of humor in Papa's voice whenever he talked about the funereal preferences of other men while ladies often went quite wild with their frocks' color palette. Through the years, I did notice Papa's occasional use of color—just the perfect touch of blue or orange, for instance—in his otherwise very dark and very dignified suits, cleverly making use of small scrap pieces that otherwise would have been thrown out without a second's thought.

He was a successful businessman. While his earnings might have been considered relatively small compared to his better-known and more aggressive rivals, his shop allowed him the luxury of saving enough to marry and start a family. The double-tragedy of losing his beloved wife and baby had driven him to work even harder, earn more, and be even more "miserly" with his money until he could afford to offer an orphaned little boy a chance at happiness and love.

For my part, I cared little for fashion in general though my interests jumped around a good deal so that by the time I began school in earnest, I still had no clear idea what I hoped to be as an adult. Papa urged me not to feel pressed into following his footsteps, and while I was grateful for his indulgence and understanding, I was also left adrift and confused on my own.

Should I be a banker? Should I be a solicitor? A schoolmaster? A physician? A botanist? As far as I was concerned, there were far too many options and only one brain in my skull with which I had to grapple whenever the question about my future plans arose.

Life carried on happily for a good spell with my needs as well as Papa's being very simple and quite basic. Frivolities were rarely ever indulged, but that was enough for us. My father's hard work and sacrifice eventually sent me to school—nothing fashionable or widely known as those schools favored by the rich and titled, of course, but a proper institution that offered its scholars a solid foundation upon which they could build their future.

As a student, I was capable enough but nowhere near impressive. I believe I managed to pass each year with favorable results but certainly nothing more. I told myself then that I was exerting myself to the best of my abilities, however short that best might be compared to my more successful and intelligent peers.

Mediocre is as mediocre does, I suppose, but I was better known in my school for my looks, which I understand I'd inherited from my unfortunate mother and perhaps even the man who raped her. Papa himself had called me exceedingly handsome while my schoolfellows did what boys confined in institutions segregated from the female sex were likely to do: court me with secret notes and invitations for a quiet walk somewhere.

Those notes unnerved me at first, and I chose to ignore them. Fortunately most of those interested were upper-classmen who decided to act on their fancy on their final year of school. It didn't take long before their own future prospects took over their daily concerns, easily pushing thoughts of dallying with a younger student out of their heads. A handful of my suitors were a year ahead of me but weren't as insistent as I at first feared. A couple of rejections aimed at the same boy led to my being left alone for the most part.

A select few continued, showering me with little gifts from home and romantic verses—including despondent ones cursing my indifference. I was then sixteen and had no idea what to do with any of them. I dared not speak a word of it in Papa's presence as well, but I managed to find a way out of my adolescent dilemma by begging to be a day student and convincing a very reluctant Papa of it.

No dormitories, no pillows under which unexpected notes could be slipped.

Dare I say it—I also flitted in and out of the school grounds like an untouchable fairy so that none of the students could catch me during a lull in activity. It grew quite tiresome after a while, but I doggedly carried on with my avoidance. I'd had plenty of experience doing such a thing as a child in the old orphanage, after all.

It certainly didn't escape Papa's notice.

"Edgar, you know very well we can afford boarding you in school," he said one evening over dinner. He watched me from across the table, his brows furrowing in worry. "You look too tired over this. Have you been having trouble in school, son? Is that why you're settling on being a day student?"

It took me a moment to come up with a reasonable answer that wasn't an all-out lie.

"Um—I don't think I'm very good being left alone with other students, Papa. I can't keep my mind on my lessons. It's hard to think around them sometimes because they get too rowdy and—and insistent," I replied, relieved that my face didn't feel overheated from prevaricating.

Papa, bless him, nodded and smiled ruefully. "I know what you mean. Boys your age are quite restless and far too energetic to sit still for two seconds together. Sometimes I wonder how I managed to survive my own school even as a day student."

My being a full-time student with boarding and all that appeared to be the pinnacle of academic life to my poor father, who wasn't born into wealth but whose family also did everything they could to ensure the children enjoyed all those advantages denied their parents and grandparents.

And so the matter was dropped, I heaved a sigh of relief while promising my father to take good care of myself and to stop working too hard and compromising my health. By the time I was seventeen, I'd mastered a reasonably smooth schedule divided between school, home, and an occasional helping hand at my father's shop.

The hopeful notes continued, the gifts piled up, and I kept my head down and studied hard. Little by little, the road to my future opened wider. Hope stirred in my breast as I once again entertained possibilities.

Then the fire happened. It broke out in the bakery next to my father's shop, the old wood easily consumed as the flames raged, and by the time help had doused the conflagration, nothing was left. A whole family of seven had died, three shops were decimated, and Papa—who tried desperately to save his livelihood—was carried off to a hospital with terrible injuries. My father was blinded, his left hand severely burned and needing amputation, and our one source of income completely gone.

I left school to be with him. At eighteen, I was now the sole breadwinner of my family, and I didn't know where to start looking, so I aimed for newspaper advertisements for ideas. That was when I first heard about Bridewater House and Rowena Fairclough.

Chapter 3

"Aren't you going to eat, young man?"

"Another moment if you please, Mrs. Murray. I'm almost done here." I rubbed my tired eyes and blinked the fog away while the candles' meager flames flickered nearby. I resolutely turned the page, however, and continued to scan the miniscule print.

"You said that a moment ago," came the pert reply. "Oh, and the moment before *that* as well. How many more moments will you need before you starve to death?"

I sighed and sat back, a bit defeated. "I was hoping to give one more page a try," I whined. I glanced up and found myself being stared down by a most disapproving housekeeper hovering at the door of my tiny bedroom. Her posture reassured me she wasn't about to give up any time soon, so I relented.

"That paper will still be there when you come back. Now come along." She waved a hand in a very commanding sort of way, and I couldn't help but obey.

I stood up and pushed my chair back, my gaze dropping one last time regretfully on the spread paper. Messages meant to sound alluring or insistent called out to me in somewhat readable text. I thought, with a sinking heart, just how much more time I was expected to spend looking over these advertisements.

In truth, I was fast running out of time all in all because Papa's savings were nearly depleted by now, and his pain-easing salves and medicines were costing us so much already. I'd already declined the doctor's requests to visit at Papa's urging—a refusal I absolutely regretted though I understood why.

Dr. Blackwood was one of my father's most loyal patrons despite the fact that he was rich enough to afford the services of a more fashionable establishment. He'd also offered to take over Papa's healing following the disaster, but even well-meaning and charitable physicians needed to be paid, and we were already close to drying up our resources.

We wouldn't be able to afford medicine, food, and even Mrs. Murray's services though she'd insisted upon staying on at a reduced pay. I needed—desperately needed—to find something immediately.

My weary gaze strayed to a somewhat lengthy help wanted posting, and I had to blink.

"WANTED, a young man of proper bearing and education for the post of secretary and personal assistant in a quiet country house. He must be able to read clearly and write with an elegant hand, follow very particular orders without question or hesitation, and patiently attend to the singular but harmless requests of an aging spinster with a cheerful and gentle disposition. The young man must be clean-shaven and excessively neat in appearance, soft-spoken, sober, and steady in character. Excellent wages for the right person. Apply for name and address at the office of this paper, etc."

How curious, I thought as I reread the advertisement a few more times, that the hopeful employer requested the services of a young man and not a young lady. Perhaps this "aging spinster" had had enough of female companions or lady's maids unless she was presently being humored by an indulgent family member. Was her memory fading and her behavior growing more eccentric? I wouldn't doubt it, but perhaps I was jumping too quickly to conclusions.

Well, the advertisement did refer to her behavior as singular but harmless. Eccentricity must be the answer to that puzzle, and the promise of excellent wages stoked my interest further.

I circled the text with my pen before picking up one candle while blowing out the flame on the other. The use of two candles was excessive, I knew, but working late into the night scouring countless advertisements for work necessitated the desperate indulgence. At least Mrs. Murray understood though I hated seeing the sympathy in her eyes when I drew closer, my stomach grumbling.

We both paused by Papa's door and peered inside. He lay fast asleep, his breaths steady but sometimes disturbed by a soft groan of pain. His heavily bandaged arm lay on his stomach, and even in the dim light of the moon piercing the curtain-less window, I could see his scarred face twisting in remembered agony. When he woke up in the morning, the tortured scrunch of features would ease into the despondent mask of a defeated man.

The good news was that his eyes were healing. The heat and smoke had momentarily affected them, but his vision would return—not as clearly as before but close enough. From what Dr. Blackwood had told us, his right eye would likely be worse than his left, but at least he'd still be able to see.

I softly closed the door and followed Mrs. Murray downstairs to the small dining-room where she'd prepared a modest but delicious meal for me. I ate in silence while she puttered around, softly humming and soothing my grieving spirits with familiar little tunes from my childhood.

I pondered the help wanted posting, turning it over and over in my head and finding reasons why I thought I was the perfect candidate for the job despite my lack of a complete education. I could read easily enough. I learned how to add feeling and excitement to a paragraph while reading it aloud in order to capture an audience's attention. My handwriting was as elegant as any, I suppose, but it was legible, and none of my teachers had ever complained.

In appearance, I reckoned I at least enjoyed a bit of an upper-hand should the decision come down to looks. Considering my remarkable experiences in school as a hoped-for sweetheart among older students, perhaps I could offer a pleasing enough countenance to an old spinster.

"Mrs. Murray," I said, "why do you suppose a lady would request the help of a gentleman?"

"In what way, dear?"

"Oh—a personal assistant of sorts? A secretary, for sure."

Mrs. Murray snorted at that but carried on with her tidying up. With economy now in full effect, our means of lighting rooms had diminished greatly, and the poor woman had to make do with a lamp she'd bought with her own wages and carried with her whenever she came. It also made her task more challenging to a point, and she was obliged to go about things more slowly than before to avoid accidents.

It was well after dinner-time, and I could tell she was tired. She should have gone home to help look after her grandchildren by now, but she insisted upon staying until I was quite done and ready for bed. In truth, I didn't know if I could ever repay her for her heartbreaking kindness.

"I'd guess she finds it a great deal easier dealing with men than women," she replied after a brief moment's thought. "I feel the same way, you know. More often than you expect, I reckon."

"You do? How come?"

"Oh, I can't say for sure. I just find it easier dealing with a man's simpler demands than a woman's. I raised five children. If I were to work for someone, I'd like that someone to be a gentleman with less demands on my time than a lady who requires too much."

I raised a brow at her. "Are you saying you're biased against your own sex?"

"Biased? Ha! I *know* my own sex, young man, and I can bravely say I *know* it too much." Mrs. Murray laughed heartily at that. "My dear, it's all a matter of personal preference. It just so happens that I prefer the less fussy company of men when I already have too much to sort out in my own home. Maybe that says terrible things about me, but I'm really too old to care."

It was my turn to laugh though the idea of feeling some dislike toward one's own sex unsettled me a little. I wondered if other ladies felt the same way toward each other.

"Why the questions, Edgar? Did you see something peculiar in the newspaper?"

"I—I thought it was peculiar," I admitted with a slight shrug. Mrs. Murray had now paused in her work and faced me, a rag in hand and eyebrows raised. "But it sounded promising enough. I mean—it sound like the sort of position I can apply for considering how little I have to offer."

I blushed at that, and her look of surprise melted into one of motherly fondness.

"You have much to offer," she replied in a quieter voice. "Don't let your father's disaster tell you otherwise. You know what I've said before about doors opening and shutting..."

I nodded and smiled tentatively. "Opportunities arising from tragedies and all that?"

"Your father suffered a horrible tragedy years ago. And look what it gave him." She walked toward me and touched my face with a work-roughened hand as she smiled, a light of wonder in her eyes. "It gave him you. And I've never seen a happier and prouder man."

"Not even your husband, Mrs. Murray?"

"Cheeky brat. Are you done yet?"

The dishes were cleaned and put away, Mrs. Murray was gone from my silent home, and I was at my father's side, ensuring his comfort and watching him sleep. I stroked his damp hair gently and thought about my prospects, determination hardening as I considered his sacrifices through the years.

"I'll make things better for us, Pa," I whispered. "I promise."

I bent down to kiss his forehead and then withdrew to my room. I stayed up another hour, planning my next move and cutting out the help wanted posting to take with me. I didn't even know where the newspaper's office was, but I could always inquire. Surely even a boy barely out of school—or, rather, unable to finish school—could manage that.

I went through my wardrobe next and chose the proper clothes though I knew none of them would be considered good enough for a successful interview. I might as well think about looking the part of a sober and respectable applicant to the newspaper people. Hopefully they wouldn't think twice about sharing the information I needed when I appeared before them, cap in hand.

My father slept in the following morning, and I didn't wake him. I asked Mrs. Murray to bring him up his breakfast when he woke up as I had to go to the newspaper office as early as I could manage.

"Good luck, dear," she said with a brilliant smile. "I'm sure you'll do well."

It didn't take me long to get the information I needed and turned my steps toward the newspaper office near the center of Bracklewhyte. An hour after breakfast I was half-stumbling about in a nervous flutter with my desired address and directions in hand.

Another half-hour followed, and I was emerging from the dark confines of newspaper offices, a little baffled as to how I managed to be coherent from start to finish. I'd never had this sort of experience before, and I was now wondering if this terrible agitation was going to be my lot whenever I sought employment. Good heavens, how often did people look for work in their lifetimes? God help me if I were to chase after a job more than twice.

And that wasn't even the real interview I was ill-prepared for. The address of the country house—a Bridewater House—was a dismaying distance from the city, and I needed to find a means of conveyance just to test my luck.

"Good heavens, Edgar," Mrs. Murray cried when I returned home looking quite harried from worry. "My Bernard will take you. He's set to arrive in the next half hour with the bread I made last night. It won't be hard to convince him to take you to Bridewater House."

I felt the blood drain away from me. "But—I can't do that! He's got work to do!"

"Indeed—work for me, you mean?" Mrs. Murray laughed and shook her head. "He's delivering bread and vegetables to my few customers day in and out, my dear. And he gets paid a proper wage for his troubles and gets fed quite well, I daresay."

Bernard was Mrs. Murray's orphaned nephew who was born with a "child-like" brain as she described his condition. But he was a bright and cheerful fellow who was friendly and quite chatty, and he never failed to raise my spirits with his colorful stories and irrepressible energy. He also appeared to be doing well enough helping his family with their own humble side business of delivering food from their flourishing garden and busy kitchen to a small scattering of cottages some distance outside Bracklewhyte.

"It's good for him to be busy and productive," Mrs. Murray had said one time, a melancholy air about her as she watched Bernard rumble off on his little rickety cart laden with loaves of bread and some vegetables from the family garden. "The poor fellow needs to learn how to be independent and survive on his own, and heaven knows, we've tried to help him find work. It's just—I'm not going to be around for him all his life, you see. And when I go, who'll take care of him?"

When Bernard appeared with that day's supply of bread, he proved Mrs. Murray right by loudly urging me to join him on the cart. "We'll both have an adventure today, Master Edgar," he said with a gap-toothed grin and a hearty slap of his thigh. "To the country we go!"

"Bah! Hardly the country, but don't get lost, you two," Mrs. Murray called out once I was settled in, and Bernard was turning the horse around. "Or I'll never hear the end of it from Mr. Cushing!"

"It will be great fun, Aunt Phyllida! I'll take care of Master Edgar! I have food!"

Bernard then pressed a piece of bread in my hand and followed it with a small chunk of cheese. I gratefully took his gifts and ate them as we rode through the city and beyond.

Chapter 4

Bridewater House might have stood "just a handful of miles away" according to the newspaper folk, but it may as well have been a hundred. The ride down the main road felt endless and tedious despite the pleasant company and frequent stops to stretch our limbs and rest our sore backsides. My heart sank when we finally turned into a side road that cut through a sparse wood—only to face another long stretch of narrow road. At least the land on which the property stood looked beautifully untamed.

The wide expanse of rather tall grass was generously littered with bursts of vivid color as flowers of an incredible variety bloomed in thick clusters throughout. It seemed as though some ancient giant once upon a time decided to fling a generous handful of seeds and left them alone to sprout and take root. And most remarkable of all, nothing was allowed to grow past a certain height. There was a very clear exercise of control in the way the wild beauty of a private field was kept within strict boundaries.

Bernard and I fell silent as we stared in bug-eyed awe at the scene around us. The wood surrounded the flower field (as I now called it), the generously spaced trees making for a gentle wall that promised romantic walks among them. I wondered how the wood looked at sunset—how everything captured and made use of the waning light.

As for the rest of the flower field and the grand house looming at the end of the long drive, there was certainly something to be said about the confidence that seemed to permeate everything around us. A quiet arrogance, even, of someone who knew precisely what they wanted and ensured the fulfillment of their desires with unfeeling, calculated exactness.

"I want everything to look *just* like this. I want the wood to surround my land *just* so. At *precisely* a mile, I want my house to stand. And I want it to face west at *exactly* the correct angle when the sun touches the distant treetops," the voice I imagined for the owner of such a marvelous property said in my head.

"Lord, Master Edgar," Bernard breathed without a break in our progress. "Looks just like a fairy tale place, doesn't it?"

I stared at the magnificent structure ahead as we neared it. "Even the house itself looks like a castle."

"Is it very old, do you think, sir?"

"I don't know," I replied. My gaze tracked the ivy climbing steadily up the gray stone walls. They clung to the masonry and appeared to race each other toward the roof. At the moment, they were grazing what I believed to be the ceiling of the ground floor. "Maybe not that old if the ivy's anything to go by."

"It sure looks old to me."

I had to chuckle at that doubtful mutter. Bridewater House certainly called to mind those amusing follies so fashionable among the wealthy who wished to have their fancy and pride stroked with architectural excesses. Papa had told me once about a lord's youngest son who scrimped on everything because he preferred to spend his money on a folly that looked like the ruins of an ancient church. His valet went to my father's shop for his (the valet's) suits, and the chatterbox proved to be a most entertaining patron. Papa used to remark just how much gossip could be shared in an hour's span.

Bridewater House was certainly not a castle though it was made to appear like one. Too small, I thought, bemused, however prettily the structure was designed and the details specifically chosen. Crenellations and four conical spires topped the building. There were only two floors, but they appeared to be built quite high. Tall windows in the old gothic style lined the walls, and I imagined those rooms to be flooded with a good deal of light during the day. All in all, the architecture of Bridewater House was modest in terms of decorative elements, but what it lacked it more than made up for in its imposing dignity.

A narrow ring of weathered stone made from the same one used on the house wrapped around the building. Every twenty-five feet or so a bench stood on the edge of the stone walk, allowing people to rest their feet and either face the house or the vast field of cheerful flowers. I imagined those benches erected along the sides of the house offered a very pretty view of the woodland. If I were hired, I'd surely take advantage of such a magnificent opportunity. Flanking each bench was a pair of stone urns topped with greenery.

A pang of pain dampened my spirits as I looked around me and took in the dreamlike environment.

"If Papa could only see all this," I murmured.

"Oh, look—someone's watching us," Bernard piped up. He elbowed me gently and pointed at one of the upper-windows. "Drat. He's gone."

"A servant, I'm sure." At this point we finally stopped the little cart, and it was all I could do to sit and gawk at the front door and its imposing knocker. Anxiety assailed me then, and I was forced to shake it off as I reminded myself of my poor father. "Well, Bernard—wish me luck."

I glanced at him and received a pleased grin as he nodded. "You'll be fine, Master Edgar. I'll wait for you here."

I clambered down the cart, straightened my jacket, and quickly tidied my hair and hat. After getting another word of encouragement from Bernard, I resolutely marched to the door and knocked. It took a handful of seconds before the door was opened, and I was staring nervously at the curious but pleasant face of the housekeeper.

"Yes?"

"Oh—good morning, ma'am. I'm here to apply for the post of secretary and personal assistant," I stammered.

"You are? Splendid! Do come in, young man. I'm Mrs. Quigg, the housekeeper." Mrs. Quigg stepped aside and then peered out. "Does your driver need refreshments? I imagine it's been a bit of a ride for both of you. My dear mistress does love her privacy, and I know it's quite trying to those who aren't used to her tastes."

Her easy solicitousness for Bernard's welfare quickly warmed me toward her, and a brief exchange with Bernard later (he refused any offers of food and insisted on waiting for me right where he'd stopped the cart), I was being led through a sumptuously decorated hallway toward the drawing-room.

"Mrs. Fairclough isn't busy this morning, thankfully. It's no trouble at all seeing you. Oh—she wishes to see you with and without your hat on." Mrs. Quigg knocked on the double doors.

"Come in!" a low and surprisingly firm voice called from within. I was then ushered inside the spacious drawing-room, my senses buffeted by the trappings of wealth currently crowding every wall and every bit of space on the floor.

Happily enough, those tall and numerous gothic-style windows allowed plenty of outside light through as I'd suspected (and, indeed, hoped). Whatever shadows might have gathered among the pieces of furniture scattered around the room were well and fully vanquished. And there, in the distant part of the drawing-room, sat Mrs. Fairclough.

She smiled as warmly as her housekeeper and welcomed me with a gentle and easy manner. After I refused an offer of tea to help ease my nerves for the interview, we proceeded with the business at hand. I discovered quite quickly just how direct the lady was—how sure and confident she was. How much control she wielded with little effort.

"So, Mr. Cushing—I'm sure my job post must have baffled you," Mrs. Fairclough said with an impish grin. She must have been a great beauty in her youth, I thought. I couldn't tell her full height because she was unfortunately limited to her loveseat, a thin shawl around her shoulders despite the warm weather and the shut windows.

Her features were almost angelic even with the wrinkles and slight shadows edging her eyes. I saw no hardness anywhere, her oval-shaped face quite soft and further softened by time's passing. Light blue eyes that reminded me more of winter than summer settled on me with a steady and inquiring gaze. There was curiosity there as well as an openness and keen intelligence that didn't judge me and my unfashionable clothes. She even appeared to be very, very interested in what I had to say in response to her questions.

"I must admit I was, ma'am," I replied.

"Put your hat on, please. Thank you. Hmm. Now take it off again. Ah—certainly much better."

Mrs. Fairclough had requested that I take the nearest window seat, which I thought to be an odd place to make me comfortable. I set my hat down on the cushioned ledge beside me and nervously fussed over my hair, which had a tendency to dip into my eyes.

"Well, you're experiencing my peculiarities right now. I asked you to sit there and not on a chair directly across from this loveseat. It's the light, you see. I wish to see how you look against it."

I nodded, my face warming as she grinned again and looked for all the world like a playful schoolgirl and not an ailing old gentlewoman.

"I'm exceedingly partial to all things theatrical, I suppose. It's simply who I am. Even when I was your age, I was causing all sorts of trouble among my parents with my pleas and demands for dramatic flourishes of—whatever happened to catch my fancy. Furniture, books, art—I've flitted from one thing to another over the years, but one thing stayed consistent, and that's my love of drama and beauty." She paused and nodded at the window behind me. "You've seen my lawn? That's another example. Unnecessarily fanciful in scope and appearance—like my castle."

She waved languidly around her, and I nodded. "Yes, ma'am."

"I need the help of a young gentleman to help counterbalance my extreme turn to dreamscapes, one might say. I need someone young enough to, of course, run particular errands for me or engage in duties requiring a good deal of focus and discipline. I'm not antagonistic toward my own sex, Mr. Cushing, though I know I sound exactly like I am."

She sighed heavily and turned her attention to the cluttered grandeur of her drawing-room. Her attention seemed to slip then which I thought was surprising given her energy and focus just a handful of seconds ago.

"It would be a most welcome change, indeed, to have another person here. Mrs. Quigg and the servants are meant to stay in the background, if you will. Out of my sight while ensuring the smooth and proper running of day-to-day affairs."

When she fell silent for a surprisingly long stretch of time, I had to clear my throat. Was she prone to distraction and reverie in the middle of a conversation like this? If so, I could see her point. She gave a light start and then turned to me with a sheepish little smile.

"What is it, dear? Have you a cup of tea yet? Shall I call for Mrs. Quigg, then?"

I shook my head and hoped I didn't look as alarmed as I felt—alarmed and sympathetic, I mean, because I was now feeling a touch of pity for the lonely old spinster. She might be wealthy and independent, but her situation must have been dearly bought, and I was now witnessing the melancholy results. Her memory appeared to be fading slowly as well, which answered a few questions I now had.

"May I ask what my duties would be, ma'am?" I prodded.

"Well—write letters as I dictate them to you, of course," she replied, the playful light back in her eyes, and she all but glowed in childish delight at the reminder of the vacant position. "A gentleman's hand is a lot less florid than a lady's, and I'm one for practicality over appearance. You'll also be reading books to me since my eyesight's not very good anymore, and my passion for good books hasn't waned a bit. Do you play a musical instrument, Mr. Cushing?"

"N—no, ma'am."

"Ah. What a pity. But you do make for a most pleasing sight sitting by the window like that. Very pretty and poetic, indeed." She paused then and then regarded me in thoughtful silence for an unnerving moment. She clasped her hands on her lap and squared her shoulders, her smile fading into something I couldn't quite read. "You must have an astonishingly beautiful mother."

"I couldn't say, ma'am, but thank you."

I could tell that poor Mrs. Fairclough was again drifting though her attention remained fixed on me. Being swept away by fancy again, I suppose. I was in fact so distracted by growing pity for her that I nearly fell off the window seat when she spoke again, and this time she gave me the amount she was willing to pay me while offering me the position. It was, in brief, a ridiculously exorbitant amount for someone with my pitiful lack of professional experience.

Once I found my voice again, I had to ask, "But—won't you be interviewing more candidates? I—I mean—surely I'm not the only suitable one."

Mrs. Fairclough waved a languid hand again. "You aren't the only one to answer my post, sir. But you *are* the best of the candidates who walked through the door." Then she sighed and leaned back in her loveseat, her girlish energy vanishing, and I was now looking at a handsome but fragile gentlewoman who had about her an air of utter defeat. "I'm dreadfully tired, Mr. Cushing. If you give me your answer now, I can have Mrs. Quigg help me back to my chamber. I don't wish to keep going with this search."

I looked around the room, took in the cluttered elegance, and thought of my father and his ruined shop. The nauseating threat of time running out pressed upon me, and I blurted out a startled "yes" before I knew what I was doing.

Chapter 5

After another moment spent sharing my history—that is, details about my family, which also touched on my unfortunate father's situation—Mrs. Fairclough evened the balance by talking about hers. Her own story was relatively innocuous by modern standards. She was an heiress who valued her independence far more than anything. Bridewater House and everything it contained was the summit of her situation in that everything about the remarkable house and its contents was exactly what she'd desired.

"Every object you see around you is me," she said once with that familiarly impish grin brightening her pale, pale face. "If the idea of immortality were to be given a physical quality, my home would be it. I daresay I'm reborn in every furniture and wallpaper and stone. They'll still be around when I'm gone, of course, which lends some amount of credence to my claim about immortality."

She was every bit as fanciful as she claimed. Her love of all things dreamlike and fairy tale-like also showed itself in her decorative choices. I imagined her to be the sort of young girl who spent much of her time lost in romantic books and art, her mind several worlds away and quite difficult to bring back to the present by practical matters.

"When I decided to lay claim to this little tract of land and build my castle, I suppose I raised several eyebrows. I inherited everything you see though perhaps the original stood in a right wretched state. Quite a dreadful eyesore—until I took over. 'Rowena,' they all said, 'what on earth are you thinking, wasting your money on such a lonely spot?' I don't have to justify my choices, Mr. Cushing. I simply follow my heart and make sure my head keeps me from straying too far into excesses." She laughed lightly at that.

I held back a grimace. She might consider her castle to be well within her limits, but to someone as poor as I, everything around me was excessive. Tastefully chosen when taken individually, yes, but cramped in one space? Yes, I suppose I'd consider that excessive. I held my tongue, of course, as one did before one's employer.

My heart lurched at the thought, and I fought back an idiotic grin. Employer. I was now contributing to my household income and supporting my father. I was useful and dependable at such a young age. My mood soared then, and it stayed ridiculously high as the remaining time was spent on idle and friendly chatter. Mrs. Fairclough clearly felt at ease with me, and she was already treating me like a friend.

The lady's predilections might be singular, to be sure, but there was nothing sinister about her manner. Her memory was clearly waning, and her energy wasn't what it used to be. However, when not distracted, she was quite sharp in her observations and unwavering in her opinions. I also thought I sensed an edge of ruthlessness in her manner whenever her mind was clear and set on the present. Oh, she didn't say or do anything terrible in my presence or in response to me. It was simply something I felt, and it was such a faint and fleeting brush against my mind that I wasn't sure there was anything there.

In the end, all doubts were easily overcome when she spoke a little more about my duties, which were really light given the incredible wage she was willing to pay me. I could entertain her with books, I could write letters in a decently attractive hand, and I could be a proper errand-boy as the situation required. On my own, I could always write to Dr. Blackwood for advice on how best to help my employer should her memory worsen, and her behavior was affected irreversibly.

I was to move in to Bridewater House once I had things settled at home, and I wasn't at all worried about Papa's welfare with Mrs. Murray fussing over him day and night. Perhaps I might even convince her to have Bernard live there, so my father could benefit from the aid and company of someone twenty-four hours a day. I could also visit on the weekends if I wished, but I couldn't stay since Mrs. Fairclough's contract required my presence at Bridewater House at all times.

I was given a month to "test the waters" and see if I could adapt as well as I could under the circumstances. At least Mrs. Fairclough understood the new and perplexing situation I now found myself. My age, my naïveté, might make my days a bit wearing given the strict control she warned me about—her insistence upon precision in the fulfillment of my duties. I was no longer a schoolboy, intent upon experiencing the world and testing its boundaries. I was given a month to get used to things.

Mrs. Quigg was called to bring in the papers for me to sign (all properly inspected and approved by Mrs. Fairclough's solicitors, of course, though the language baffled me), and a handshake later, I was back on the cart with an excited Bernard.

"You're a proper secretary now, Master Edgar!" he crowed as we rode down the drive. The midday sun flooded the gorgeous area with so much light that seemed to exaggerate the glorious colors around us.

"I hope to be a good one," I said with some hesitation. Doubts crept out again, and the threat of intimidating prospects reared its head. Was I capable of doing what the lady required? I couldn't help but wonder about that fleeting sense of ruthlessness. The reminder made me shudder a little, but in the brilliant light of the sun, the memory rent and fluttered off in all directions.

Nonsense, I thought. Stuff and nonsense.

"What will you be doing?"

I indulged my companion, who was so endearingly pleased on my account. We then talked about what wonders lay hidden behind each door of Mrs. Fairclough's castle—wonders I was about to discover and perhaps write home about.

I thought about keeping a journal so I could record every day's adventures. I expected to be living a relatively quiet existence there, and perhaps I could persuade my employer to allow me an occasional ramble through the wood and whatever land stretched past them. I imagined charming old cottages and a rolling countryside littered with sheep. On our way to Bridewater House, in fact, I glimpsed a few of those rustic homes shyly peeking out from behind hedgerows.

"Will you be playing with the children as well?"

I blinked. "Children? I didn't see any when I was inside."

"I thought I saw one looking out of one of the upper-windows," Bernard replied with a lazy shrug. "He was gone when I glanced up, though. I think it was the same one who watched us come."

I nodded at that. "Perhaps one of the servants' child. Mrs. Fairclough's a spinster, and she told me outright she never planned for a family of her own." I considered further. "I have a feeling she's also the last of her line."

I wondered then if surrounding herself with excesses had anything to do with the inevitable end and the fact that she had no one to whom she could bequeath her property and money. She did refer to her home as her second self. If she truly believed in immortality, Bridewater House would be hers for as long as it continued to stand, its foundation secure.

I shook off any moody thoughts about death and what came after when movement far up ahead drew my attention back to the present.

"Oh, look, Master Edgar," Bernard piped up. "See, Mrs. Fairclough's got another visitor. Maybe he's another fellow who's answering her job post. Isn't that wonderful? He's too late!"

"Maybe he isn't. I'd hate to be the one to disappoint him," I said, grimacing.

The newcomer was a gentleman in a thick, dusty coat, his hat equally well-used and battered and clearly one used when he needed to ride to distant places. His horse was a magnificent creature, its coat gleaming beautifully in the sun. As horse and rider drew near, I saw the gentleman's features more clearly.

A young fellow, I thought, though most likely a few years older than I. The shadows cast by his hat's brim did little in hiding his face from scrutiny—for which I was secretly grateful because he was a strikingly handsome fellow. I only managed a glimpse, wholly conscious of the rudeness of staring so blatantly, and what I caught in that too-brief span was awfully pleasant. He smiled a little as we drew near, nodding and touching his battered old hat in greeting.

"Good morning, gentlemen," he said in a very mannered way.

"Good morning!" Bernard cried most energetically.

When the gentleman's gaze settled on me, I touched my hat as well. "Good morning," I said though I was sure my voice was too tiny to be heard above the rattling wheels and scraping hooves.

I tried not to stare too much, but I did catch large-ish saddlebags on the horse. The newcomer was there on business, I assumed, relieved at the thought that I just didn't wish a rival a pleasant morning. As we turned onto the main road and picked up speed to get back to town, I chided myself for overthinking so many things back there. What did it really matter what that gentleman was going to do at Bridewater House? Why fret over things that might not even be true?

Nerves, I told myself, rubbing my arms distractedly. It must be nerves following such a remarkable and baffling interview. Everything had gone so quickly and smoothly that I wondered if Mrs. Fairclough was quite desperate to fill the vacancy. That she'd give it to someone with nothing to offer in experience and talent only served to add credence to my suspicion that she was at her wits' end after so many other applicants before me.

Her health was failing. I could see that quite well. Her mind was, too. I only hoped her decline wasn't too fast and extreme, but if nothing could be done about her health, I'd try all in my power to ensure she was comfortable and happy to the very end.

Well, that was assuming my performance was good enough for her to keep me on indefinitely, or course.

"You're thinking too hard, Master Edgar. Let's go home and celebrate your good fortune. Well—I have to finish delivering Aunt Phyllida's bread and vegetables, but I'll bring something back for us to eat," Bernard said. He snapped the reins and urged the horse to go even faster.

"It's been a very confusing morning, that's for sure," I cried, laughing. "Slow down! There's no need to rush!"

When he finally let me off at my home and left for his, I found Papa sitting up and looking quite alert in his bedroom. With Mrs. Murray in the room with us, I recounted my morning adventures and laid out the plan I spun regarding Papa's welfare. It was difficult to read my poor father's expressions given the tightness of his drawn features, but he managed a smile. He even clasped one of my hands with his good one, bringing it to his face for a firm kiss.

"I'm proud of you, Edgar," he said in a quiet and raspy voice. Dr. Blackwood said his voice would be quite ragged for a while, but like his eyes, it would heal as well. "I couldn't have asked for anything better, but—are you sure about this post?"

I colored. "I know I'm not even done with school, Papa, but I can still learn quickly enough. And the duties Mrs. Fairclough laid out for me are so light and easy to do. She can teach me how to be a proper gentleman and a good secretary. When I move on to another post in the future, at least I'll have the proper experience and skills by then."

My father listened with that fond, indulgent smile of his. "Of course. Everyone has to start somewhere. I had to learn on my own as well—watching your grandfather day in and day out, making so many mistakes along the way."

"I'll ask to come home for visits, of course."

"Of course, son."

Papa chuckled and rolled his eyes at me then, and I sighed. I hated the thought of leaving him so abruptly when he was still in desperate need of help and attention. But Mrs. Murray had agreed to my scheme involving Bernard, her own anxiety over the poor fellow mitigated somewhat by the new role he was set to play.

At least with my astonishing wages, I'd be able to afford compensating him properly despite Mrs. Murray's insistence that Bernard's pay ought to be negotiated given our two families' closely tied histories. I'd fret over that eventually, of course, because given the limited time I now had with my father, I needed to pour all energy and thought into his healing.

Mrs. Fairclough expected me to move into Bridewater House by Friday, and today was Tuesday. I barely had any time left with Papa, and I was determined to make it as cheerful and comforting to him as possible. Bernard made good his promise, and he came by at just past four in the afternoon, his arms laden with more bread and cheese. We told him about his new position as my father's nurse and companion, and he all but danced with his aunt in the tiny kitchen before bursting into tears and shaking my hands fervently.

"I'll take good care of Mr. Cushing, sir," he said over and over. "I promise he'll soon forget he's ever had you." Cheeky sod.

Chapter 6

My hours at home shrank while my nerves worsened. By the time Thursday came around, I was a bit of a mess, much to my father's amusement.

"Edgar, you'll do fine," he said, grinning over the bowl of soup I'd brought up for him. At least he was able to move around with little help though I suspected he did so for my benefit. He must still be in so much pain but dared not betray anything to me. "You're not that far away, and you're coming home for visits. Just—make sure to send us word before you do, eh? Mrs. Murray would tear the whole of Bracklewhyte down if you were to come home and nothing was prepared."

I chuckled at the picture of our dear Mrs. Murray doing just that and then sighed, shaking my head. "I know, Papa. I'm just so nervous about all this. My first job and all that, you know?"

"Yes, I do. And what I said still holds true. You'll be fine." Papa paused for a moment to observe me in thoughtful silence. "Are you regretting your decision, son?"

I sighed then and dropped my gaze to his ruined, bandaged stump resting on the blanket. "I don't regret taking the job, but I'm so terrified I'll be such a disappointment. Then I'll be tossed out on my backside, and then what?"

My father blinked, confounded. "Now what on earth made you think you'll be a disappointment? Edgar Robert Cushing, I raised you far better than that. Use this chance as a learning tool—not just new skills that can benefit you later on, but also learn about yourself. What you're truly capable of. I'm sorry you're thrown into this so suddenly and in such a drastic way, but one thing we Cushings pride ourselves in, son, is our ability to pick ourselves up, dust ourselves off, and carry on in spite of everything."

He carefully and with some effort moved his bowl to the nightstand in order to take one of my hands in his only good one for a proper squeeze. I nodded, my throat tight, at the sight of pure love and pride in his partly ruined eyes.

"I'd move heaven and earth to turn back time, Edgar," he said in a softer, gentler voice, his eyes suddenly bright with unshed tears. "I'd see you in school—see you finish and pursue further education if Heaven willed it. I'd see you go even further following years of dedication and hard work. I'd see you settled down comfortably when my time finally comes." He squeezed my hand again. "I'd move heaven and earth to see you happy, son."

"I know. I promise to work doubly hard."

"That's my boy. Now then—how about a bit of practice, Edgar?"

With a grin, my father produced a battered old book for me to read to him, and with a chuckle, I accepted the challenge.

I spent the rest of my evening in his company and waited till he drifted off, and I took his empty bowl and cup away. At least his appetite was good in spite of everything. I reminded myself to do well on his account the way I used to as a student fumbling my way through class after class. This time, however, the stakes were a great deal higher and most certainly more real.

Bernard had already moved in, taking the little storage room next to my bedroom after we hastily cleaned it out and converted it for his use. He didn't complain about the Spartan quality of his new lodgings, bless him, and he'd at least be well within earshot should Papa need his help at any time. Mrs. Murray had taken the burden of delivering bread and vegetables off his hands, and by the time I set off for Bridewater House, she'd yet to decide on how best to carry on her side business.

"Lord, child, don't fret over me!" she cried, laughing, as I all but wrung my hands before her when she confessed to the momentary pause in business. "Just go and make the world fall in love with you so your poor father won't need to worry on your account."

I reminded myself as well that I'd at least have the ability to pay her most handsomely to compensate for her sudden dip in fortune. What a terrible thought it was to have such power as to affect the lives of not just my father, but others as well.

Bernard drove me to Bridewater House immediately after breakfast, chatting all the way as was his wont and raising my spirits as he often did with his irrepressible personality. He fed me again, this time with a generous piece of gingerbread Mrs. Murray had made specifically for the occasion.

We took our time on the road and opted for longer breaks. I suppose in my defense I simply couldn't find it in myself to let Bernard go—at least not yet. Parting from him and his humble little pony and trap meant parting from familiarity and comfort.

"She's been practicing, you know," Bernard said with a pleased nod as he watched me bite into the wonderfully spiced treat. "Not just ordinary bread now, she says. Aunt Phyllida wants to master cakes because her customers keep bothering her with pleas for sweet, indulgent stuff."

Needless to say, I was quite grateful to Mrs. Murray's customers for pushing the issue. I'd always thought of her as a marvelous cook and had enjoyed her simple offerings of bread over the years, but the gingerbread was quite the revelation.

Before long my mood dipped again at the sight of the long drive and spacious woodland marking Mrs. Fairclough's property. We drove through as before, and I was soon standing in forlorn silence at the doorstep, my two bags by my feet, my eyes fixed on the receding forms of Bernard, his trap, and his pony.

I never had the chance to calm myself down when the door opened before I could knock, and Mrs. Quigg's smiling face appeared.

"Heavens, Mr. Cushing, I wondered if you'd ever knock," she cried as I huffed and grunted, carrying my bags across the threshold. "I saw your cart approach and waited. Are you nervous? Oh, don't be! You'll do splendidly, I'm sure! Now come along, sir. Let me show you to your room first."

All was silent in Bridewater House as Mrs. Quigg led me up the grand staircase and its graceful, heavily ornamented balustrade and bifurcated design. I'd barely given the magnificent structure any thought the day I first came for my interview, but now that I was a part of the household, I had the luxury of time as I marveled at every architectural flourish. Mrs. Fairclough had, indeed, spared no expense to ensure her house—her castle—perfectly fulfilled her specifications.

The landing boasted a pair of life-sized statues made to look like marble sculptures from antiquity. The two smaller, diverging flights of stairs were no less ostentatiously designed, and Mrs. Quigg led me up the left flight. Every wall groaned with the weight of exceedingly large portraits in thick frames, and after a few curious glances, I was soon struck by the realization that every one of those portraits was of Mrs. Fairclough in some form or other.

The lady appeared by herself in about half of them and was artfully posed and dressed in a variety of costumes. The rest were of her in costume and either cavorting with mythical creatures in a picturesque field or alone and lost in some activity such as reading, sewing, or playing a musical instrument. I blinked as I walked past the portraits, wondering just how many of them graced the walls of Bridewater House.

Mrs. Fairclough, in those paintings, was young—quite girlish, almost—which made me wonder just how old those things were.

As we walked down a somewhat dim passageway, I saw that the portraits were at least reasonably spaced from each other so that the relentless bombardment of Mrs. Fairclough's likeness didn't seem quite so obvious. Formal portraits were also hung in alternating fashion with the more fantastical scenes. Now and then a statue would also make a silent appearance, usually standing guard between doors. I decided they were all statues of nymphs though perhaps no two of them were alike.

Mrs. Quigg led me to a room at the end of the hallway, which she opened with a delighted grin. "Here you are, Mr. Cushing. Mrs. Fairclough herself chose this room specifically for you. Corner rooms are the best lit as you can see, and she believes having so much light pouring through those windows will be good for—well, inspiration! Are you a creative sort, sir?"

"Uh—no, ma'am. I do appreciate a good book, though."

I couldn't believe the size of my assigned room. It was easily three times the size of my old bedroom with a great deal of light streaming through the tall windows. The perpendicular walls of the corner room allowed five, with three of them staring out at the front half of the property while two faced the side.

As with the front, the narrower tract of land running past the side of the house was generously peppered with colorful flowery clusters and bordered with the same wood and its widely spaced trees. Beyond the wood stretched low, undulating terrain and more trees with nary a cottage in sight.

Bridewater House was very much an isolated, dreamscape-like sanctuary. The amazing portraits and mythological statues may be two of its most peculiar qualities, but in location, it was truly unmatched as far as I could tell.

My bedroom was just as "well-stocked" as the drawing-room in that the bed, the wardrobe, the washstand, and the writing-desk and chair were all quite huge and beautifully carved, stained, and polished. The floor boasted intricately woven rugs, and a generously sized ottoman invited endless hours spent lost in books. The canopy bed looked more intimidating and an object to gawk at than to sleep in, I thought with an involuntary shiver, because of the ridiculously decorated posts, headboard, and tester.

"How old is everything in this room, Mrs. Quigg?" I stammered as I gazed around me. I didn't remember putting my bags down, but I apparently did though it was more likely I'd simply dropped them in shock when I entered the room.

"Oh, who knows, young man?" she replied with a hearty bark of laughter. "Mrs. Fairclough is quite the collector, and each room has been furnished with deliberate care." She waved a hand around her. "Each piece means something and was chosen to tell some sort of story when considered alongside everything else in the room."

"I see. And—what does this room tell us?"

Mrs. Quigg laughed again, this time winking playfully at me while touching the side of her nose. "Ah—that's for you to find out, Mr. Cushing. Your being assigned to this room is just as deliberate, and I'm not just talking about plentiful light and inspiration."

A wave of helpless wonder washed over me as I inched closer to the bed and stared in astonishment at the gorgeously carved wood of the nearest pillar. I didn't dare touch it despite the temptation because it felt more like being in the presence of some immortal being that could easily smite me in a breath.

"If it's any comfort, I don't know the answer to that, either," Mrs. Quigg piped up from behind me. "Mrs. Fairclough can be a bit of a riddle as well considering all her fanciful notions of what to surround herself with. I daresay you've already had a taste of her eccentricities during your interview."

I nodded and turned around to smile at her sheepishly.

"Anyway, make yourself comfortable, sir. Mrs. Fairclough's currently resting and won't be up and about till noon. She'll be joining you for lunch, of course, but you've got the rest of the morning to rest and sort yourself out."

"Thank you, Mrs. Quigg. Um—where's the dining room, by the bye?"

She gave me easy enough directions, and as she was about to step out of my room, she snapped her fingers and turned around again. "I quite forgot! Mrs. Fairclough would like you to gather flowers from the property."

Flowers? I blinked. "Oh. Very well. Does she need them before or after lunch?"

"Before. You're to give the bundle to me, and I'll be putting them together in a proper arrangement for dinner." She waited for my reply, which was a quick and wordless nod, before adding, "She also wants a variety of flowers in violet, please. Every possible shade you can find of the color, so you've got the freedom to walk around and cover as much ground as you can—but only from the front."

The distant sound of the clock chiming cut through her talk, and she appeared to count the doleful sounds in silence. Once the clock stopped, she smiled at me again. "It's ten o'clock, so if you could be downstairs by eleven, I can provide you with a basket for your task."

Not much time left for me to make myself comfortable, I thought, but it didn't matter. I was now being tasked to do something quite specific for my employer, and I could always rest later. With an answering smile and another wordless nod, I was finally left alone.

I went about unpacking my bags and carefully putting things in their proper places when I thought I heard a quiet knock on my door. I hurried to open it and was surprised to find no one there. I stepped out into the hallway and looked around, even calling out "Mrs. Quigg? Is that you?" and receiving no answer. With a shrug, I shut the door and went back to putting my things away. Large, fanciful houses made just as much noise as any other house, I suppose.

Chapter 7

Violet flowers of varying shades and only those from the front of the property, I thought, somewhat perplexed. The basket Mrs. Quigg gave me was large enough for my task, and she also kindly provided me with a pair of shears. I didn't have gloves, however, which meant I needed to be very careful and look twice before handling anything.

The late morning sun was wonderfully pleasant and warm enough to make me sweat a little as I picked my way from one violet cluster to another. The field of grass and flowers soothed me, the fresh air cleaned my lungs, and the occasional birdsong encouraged me to sink happily into fanciful thoughts. Grass and dirt clung to my trousers and jacket, and I had to pause now and then to wipe sweat off my brows.

Mrs. Quigg didn't give me instructions on how many flowers I was expected to gather, but I decided to fill the basket all the same. If a flower arrangement were to be the fruit of my efforts, I should make it as theatrical as possible. I was sure Mrs. Fairclough would love it.

I'd reached the halfway point of the "wilderness garden" as I now called it when a horse and rider appeared at the entrance of the drive and idly trotted toward the house. I was then on my knees, the tall grass grazing my elbows, the basket of cut flowers beside me. I'd just finished cutting a few more blooms from the gently hued cluster when the newcomer appeared.

He stopped his horse just as I glanced up and met his curious gaze. It was, I realized, the same gentleman who passed me and Bernard as we drove out of the property. This time we locked gazes for a longer stretch of time, and I took hold of the opportunity to observe and admire.

"Good morning again," he said, a smile lighting his handsome features. "Tell me, are you Mrs. Fairclough's family?"

"No, sir," I replied. He spoke with a lovely accent, I thought. I also didn't know till then just how much a most attractive stranger's attention could freeze my extremities so that I couldn't even move from my awkward position in the middle of the grass. "I'm her new assistant."

I'd been told by Mrs. Fairclough herself to refer to myself as her "assistant" because "secretary" was too limiting and stodgy while "personal assistant" sounded a touch improper. But the lady's singular turns really shouldn't surprise me in spite of my newness to all this, and I had to remind myself to simply go along with her wishes.

"I see. I remember seeing you on your way out a few days ago."

"Yes—I—uh—I'd just finished my interview for the job."

He nodded, his steady and assessing gaze making me squirm a little, and I had to break his hold on me by forcing myself to look down at the basket.

"Mrs. Fairclough asked me to gather violet flowers for a dinner-time floral arrangement," I offered rather weakly. I was quite sure my face was tomato red by then.

"She did, did she?" He chuckled and then sighed. "I wouldn't be surprised if your flowers will eventually find their way in her next portrait."

I blinked. "You've noticed them, then? The portraits, I mean?"

"How can anyone *not* notice them?" he replied, laughing. "I've only managed a few watercolor studies for now that I've yet to put to canvas, and Heaven only knows how many more she's got planned. Her ideas come a great deal faster than I can wield a brush, I'm afraid." He pinned me with another keen and thoughtful gaze before nodding smartly. "Well, I'll leave you to your task, monsieur. We'll be meeting again within doors soon enough."

I nodded as well, abashed by the bold scrutiny, and I was watching horse and rider move toward the house, the sound of the front door opening before they even reached it indicating the newcomer's easy welcome and expected appearance. Mrs. Quigg appeared to guide the gentleman in while a fellow I'd yet to meet—a groom, I supposed—led the horse toward the back of the house. Then all was again silent and soothing though at this point my turn to fanciful distraction had evaporated fully, my mind now filled with a handsome French artist.

I wandered a little aimlessly through the flower field for a few minutes longer. Every now and then I'd glance back at the house, a touch puzzled, because I thought I felt the weight of someone's eyes upon me. But all I managed to catch were tall, empty windows all perfect rows. Perhaps it was just an effect of being in the sun for too long, I reckoned, and ignored the strange feeling—to no avail, sadly. At length I had to shake myself impatiently and direct my steps back to the house.

I didn't meet the gentleman when I entered, which I thought was a stroke of luck because I felt quite dirty and smelly from all that time outside. It didn't take me long to find Mrs. Quigg and surrender my basket. I still had around fifteen minutes left before I was expected in the dining room for lunch, and I hastened up the stairs to my room so I could wash and change.

I scrubbed myself as thoroughly as I could with a wet cloth, stripping completely and ensuring every inch of my skin was cleared of sweat, sun, and dirt. I saved the rest of the water in the ewer for later as I didn't know if I could ask for more. I peered at myself in the mirror once I was once again dressed, my hair combed as neatly as it allowed me, anyway.

"Lord, behave!" I hissed. My hair never listened. I suppose my age made me a touch vain because I spent more time fussing over my rebellious hair than my clothes, earning myself endless hours of teasing from Mrs. Murray (who cut my hair fashionably short and taught me how best to keep my face clean and free of "ugly whiskers", toward which she'd always harbored an unusual amount of loathing).

Despairing blue eyes peered back at me from the depths of the mirror, and I had to resign myself to somewhat unruly hair in Mrs. Fairclough's presence. With a dismal sigh I tidied up the washstand and folded my dirty clothes, placing them on the foot of the bed for the time being.

I turned to leave and then froze.

"What..."

I looked back at the bed and realized I wasn't imagining things. A little wooden soldier lay on the covers near the foot of the bed, just a few inches shy of my clothes. I stared at the toy in confusion at first because I could have sworn the bed had nothing on it when I put my things away earlier. I remembered even running my hand in wonder over the covers, marveling at their softness and impressive design.

"Where on earth did you come from?" I murmured as I picked up the toy and inspected it closely.

It appeared to be quite old, the wood and painted details somewhat worn and chipped off in places. A child must have loved it, enjoyed playing with it for some time judging from the amount of wear it sported. And other than those details, I saw nothing else that made it stand out—no name carved into the wood anywhere.

"Perhaps one of the servants' children?"

I scratched my head and then pocketed it as I doubted my memory. I could have sworn the toy wasn't there when I stripped, but then again, my earlier exertions must have muddled my brain into chasing after odd things. I should pursue the matter later when I was free, I told myself, and with any luck, Mrs. Quigg would be able to identify the toy for me.

I entered the dining-room at precisely twelve, and there I found Mrs. Fairclough already seated at the table with the French gentleman keeping her company. They were in the middle of a lively conversation—their laughter being easily heard even as I descended the stairs—when I entered.

"Ah! There he is at last!" Mrs. Fairclough cried, grinning at me and waving me in. She was in very high spirits this time, quite the opposite of her delicate and fading state when she interviewed me. With her mood and energy so buoyed, she called to mind those fantastical portraits of her. "Come in, Mr. Cushing, come in. We don't stand on ceremony here, do we, M. Boivin?"

"Indeed, we don't, Madame." M. Boivin rose from his chair as I approached the table hesitantly, his eyes once again fixed upon me and rendering me quite stupid.

"This is Edgar Cushing, my new assistant," Mrs. Fairclough said. "Mr. Cushing, may I introduce Cyrille Boivin, artiste extraordinaire?" She laughed brightly again, her low, melodic voice taking on a giddy and childish quality as M. Boivin walked around the table with his hand outstretched. "His family goes back, you know—his father, uncle, and grandfather were commissioned paint and sculpt for me once upon a time when I was a mere slip of a girl. And now it's young M. Boivin's turn."

"A pleasure to meet you, monsieur," M. Boivin said, his voice dropping to a murmur as we shook hands. "Please call me Cyrille. Mrs. Fairclough is correct when she said we don't stand on ceremony."

"Of course. Then please call me Edgar."

"Edgar it is." His hold lingered a little, his smile softening, and then he released me and returned to his seat just as Mrs. Quigg appeared with one of the maids, both carrying trays of roast meat, boiled vegetables, and bread.

I was sure my face stayed awfully red the whole time we ate though I barely spoke and took to listening to my companions. They were far more comfortable in each other's presence, naturally, having enjoyed a longer relationship as artist and patroness. I answered a few questions aimed my way and was pleased to see Mrs. Fairclough too caught up with talking about her plans for expanding her art indoors to notice my reticence.

Cyrille behaved as gentlemanly as ever but was also on friendly terms with the lady, his manner easy and open and almost brotherly when they teased each other.

"The flowers you picked are still with Mrs. Quigg, my dear," Mrs. Fairclough said after a brief lull in conversation. "Oh—you'll find my slipping in manners sometimes, I'm afraid. If I call you 'my dear' now and then, do ignore the boldness. I try to be more dignified in my dealings with my household, but your role is quite different from the others.'"

"I don't mind, ma'am," I stammered. "This is my first job, and I'm here to learn from you and M. Boivin as well."

"You'll see I'm not as formidable as you might have thought at first. Indeed, I prefer to treat you like family. M. Boivin, of course, is on a friendlier but still professional footing. You don't mind, do you, my dear? Our lovely artistic guest certainly doesn't."

"I understand, ma'am. I don't mind at all."

She grinned, her pale features looking even more angelic and perfect as the years seemed to vanish. "Then from this day forward, I expect you to call me Rowena."

I stared at her and then at Cyrille, who merely drank from his glass without taking his heavy gaze off me. I looked at her again. "But—I can't, Mrs. Fairclough. I—I work for you."

"And it's your job to do as I tell you, is it not? So call me Rowena, please. Mrs. Fairclough is what Mrs. Quigg and the others use, and I prefer to be more like an older relation to you."

"Go on, Edgar," Cyrille piped up. "No harm done if the lady requests it."

"Well—all right. I'm sorry. I've never—"

Rowena cut me off with a languid wave of a hand. "You've never been in this position before, yes, yes, yes. No need to repeat yourself, dear. Now eat. We've a full day ahead of us."

I fell silent and sank back in my chair while Rowena picked up where she and Cyrille had left off in their conversation. Mortified beyond words, I stayed quiet for the rest of the meal though still managed to enjoy the delicious fare.

Was this how the moneyed class behaved? Perhaps in some circles, niceties and propriety were disposed of, and no one would bat an eye since wealth justified eccentricities.

I didn't know what to think, in truth, and I wished I had more time to get myself more settled in Bridewater House so as to be able to weather Rowena's odd turns more easily. I found her insistence on overly familiar addresses to be unsettling, and even Cyrille's ready defense of her behavior didn't sit well, but what did I know?

And as the meal progressed and conversation between them carried on, I comforted myself with thoughts of Papa and how well he'd be provided for from now on. I simply needed to exercise patience and forbearance toward a gentlewoman who'd had her way for so long now that any sour thoughts about her would be shameful. She was, after all, nearing the twilight of her years, and if all the ostentatious displays of vanity inside her home were any indication, her strange turns were harmless.

I was reluctantly drawn back to the conversation when Cyrille asked me about my tastes in art. I answered with my usual pathetic knowledge of great works, which in turn drew a rather gallant offer to help me learn more about his heroes. Quite a few names were dropped, and my head hurt from a mad struggle to keep up with all references to Rembrandt and Caravaggio and Poussin, among others.

"Oh, perhaps my next sitting should be something like a Vermeer," Rowena cried, turning to Cyrille. "What do you think, sir? I shall have a proper costume made. A private, domestic scene would be perfect, don't you agree? With orange and yellow flowers picked by Edgar worked in somewhere. I love orange and yellow and how they represent energy and life in a furious explosion."

Yet another offering to the altar of immortality, I couldn't help but think, my glance resting on a nearby portrait of Rowena dancing heedlessly with a group of shepherdesses in a brightly lit meadow.

Chapter 8

Rowena withdrew in order to dress for that afternoon's sitting while Cyrille led me to the studio. It was, as it turned out, located just behind the grand staircase, directly across the separating wall. And that wall boasted two more nymph statues flanking a particularly large portrait of Rowena in the most extravagant dress—one fit for a royal ball, I wagered.

She posed as though she were royalty, to be sure, standing tall and proud with her chin raised and her gaze bold and even challenging. And from where it hung, it seemed as though Rowena kept an imperious eye on the comings and goings of the studio.

Cyrille swept right inside with long, confident strides while I trailed in his shadow, my eyes boggling and my mouth hanging open most idiotically.

"Behold, my kingdom within someone else's," he declared with a burst of laughter. He waved a hand around. "My studio enjoys a great deal of light, and there's that door over there leading to the outside. On warm days I leave it and the windows open for a bit of fresh air because—clearly, I've need for it."

The smell of paint and turpentine was rather strong, I thought, wrinkling my nose as I moved idly among canvases stacked against each other or, in the case of those partly used, propped up on an old easel or leaning against a wall. Rags and large pieces of stained cloth littered the floor, catching spills and accidents, I suppose. I was actually surprised Rowena had allowed such a thing in her pristine home. I'd have expected her to have a prettily designed studio built independently of the house, standing somewhere in the grounds.

In addition to canvases, there were also a couple of sizable sideboards standing on opposite sides of the studio, each nearly overrun by books and sheets of paper Cyrille had sketched on. I wondered what the sideboards' drawers held and wouldn't be surprised if more artistic tools and equipment were kept in them.

The room on the whole appeared to be very well used with its topsy-turvy contents and creative messes. Cyrille took his place in the center of the studio where his easel stood, a blank canvas sitting on it. Directly across from the easel stood a bust a woman wearing a tall, elaborate wig from the previous century.

"This is marvelous," I breathed as I observed the room. I glanced up at the walls and found none of them embellished with art, curiously enough. On one of the sideboards a haphazardly stacked pile of watercolor studies sat, and with Cyrille's pleased nod, I went through them in breathless awe.

"These are beautiful! And they're only studies? They ought to be properly framed and displayed!"

"Thank you. I must admit I'm quite proud of them."

"As you should be. How lovely—the colors—I notice you use a fairly muted palette."

"Mrs. Fairclough's preference, which, I'm happy to say, aligns with mine."

I continued my slow walk around the studio and paused before the bust, staring at it in some confusion. It sat on a pedestal of elegantly designed dark wood. I forced myself to keep my hands away from everything in the room though my fingers itched to touch and explore.

"Who's this?" I asked, turning to find Cyrille just about finishing buttoning his artist's smock.

"Not really sure. Nobody if you ask me, but Mrs. Fairclough prefers to see it as Marie Antoinette." Cyrille grinned with a mischievous twinkle in his eyes. He then proceeded to gather his brushes and rags, half of which had apparently fallen to the ground. "I'm set to paint her dressed as a shepherdess from last century, posing by the bust."

I stared at him. "Whatever on earth for?"

"Because I want to, of course. What a silly question, my dear," a voice bright with laughter answered from the direction of the doors, and Rowena sailed right inside the studio, fully dressed like a shepherdess.

She had on the sort of clothes I suspected rustic girls wore while tending their flock, but as I'd never seen any real shepherdesses or depictions of them in art (outside poetry, I mean), I couldn't tell if what she used was accurate. She'd gathered her hair and secured it under a large straw hat. Her white blouse was quite voluminous and secured tightly around her chest and waist with stays cinched with colorful ribbons. Her apron and skirt also looked quite fine and elegantly designed, and the longer I looked at her costume, the more I was convinced the dress was meant to flatter her form more than convey a harsher and less forgiving life working exposed to the elements.

Well, I suppose that was the purpose of these portraits, I thought as I watched her take her place beside the bust with a pleased and triumphant air about her.

"I'm ready, M. Boivin," she said. "Let's get on with the sketches first."

"Almost there, Madame," Cyrille replied. I stepped aside and placed some distance between myself and the two, wondering where I should situate myself.

"Oh—Edgar, I've just inspected the flowers you gathered for this evening's table setting. I expect you to do the same but with another color tomorrow," Rowena said as she turned to me.

"Very well," I stammered. Were my first few days about to be spent gathering flowers for the table?

As Cyrille walked to one of the sideboards for something, Rowena continued, "In the meantime, do acquaint yourself with Bridewater House. This is your first day with us, and since I'm about to be engaged for a while, it would do you good to get comfortable around here."

"Yes, ma'am," I replied as I inched my way to the door.

It was then when I noticed just how cold the studio was. There was an unused fireplace that had been screened off, thankfully. I sincerely doubted if anyone thought it a clever idea to light a fire with the air quite soaked with the smell of paint and turpentine.

A shudder rippled through me at the memory of the fire that had destroyed so many lives though I also couldn't help but wonder if that involuntary response was also because of the studio's startlingly chilly temperature. A breeze was now blowing through the rear door and into the studio, and it was a pleasantly warm one but still didn't make much of a difference in regulating the temperature within.

Rowena and Cyrille didn't seem to mind, or at least they seemed to be so used to it that they didn't notice anything amiss.

"Oh, and before I forget," Rowena said just as I reached the doorway, "I'd like you to read to me during tea. Go to the library upstairs and find a good book that you think is suitable for an afternoon of quiet entertainment. I'll expect you to be in the drawing-room in two hours."

"Well—have you any preferences, ma'am?" I grimaced when Rowena's smile faltered and her face hardened at my use of "ma'am" for the second time, but she quickly gathered herself.

"Surprise me, Edgar. Go on now. I'm quite busy here." Rowena dismissed me with her usual languid hand-wave, and she proceeded to pose beside the bust while Cyrille directed her using his painting as a guide.

I went upstairs and decided to tarry a bit in my room. Vanity had taken full hold of me then, and I fussed over my appearance with my comb and a damp towel. I wasn't expected to appear before my employer for another two hours, and I now wondered what else I could do with myself besides hunt down a book. I scanned my room and thought about improvements I could make, which also meant bringing books there as well for my personal reading pleasure.

The library itself wasn't as expansive as the studio, and it could only be accessed through one set of large double-doors. I ran into no one during my wanderings, and the upper floor was awfully silent. The rear hallway only had rooms running along one side, the opposite wall sporting those magnificent windows from end to end, all facing the back part of the flower field and woodland. Those stone nymphs lined the walls in between the rooms as expected, while more portraits of Rowena in fantastical environments hung in alternating sequences in between the tall windows.

I couldn't help but pause before the library doors and observe the silent and brightly lit hallway, wondering about the oddities of the house's layout and design. That said, it really felt as though I were standing in a grand castle of sort, looking down in childish wonder at a long hallway awash with light on one side and richly embellished with elegant statuary, paintings, and furniture on the other.

Then again, I suppose Bridewater House itself was one architectural idiosyncrasy accurately reflecting its mistress's peculiar nature. It was a dreamscape come to life, and that was simply that. Being in the middle of everything made me feel as though I were also a part of Rowena's growing collection.

Like the studio below it, the library doors were also left open, and entering the room felt like being transported to some magical realm. Unlike the studio below, the library was octagonal in design, which I thought lent the room a very cozy and calming feel because it felt as though I were being embraced by hundreds of books.

Bookshelves packed with volumes of every size and thickness lined every wall, and they all reached at least twelve feet in height overall. Each wall of shelves had its own rolling ladder boasting exquisite scroll-work in wrought iron while the shelves themselves were all of the same heavy, carved, and polished dark wood. An armchair stood near one side while a chaise longue stood across the way from it. Two small tables upon which sat exquisite candelabras were paired with the furniture. Plump pillows were artfully placed on the armchair and the chaise longue, excesses spilling onto the floor in an inviting cluster. There was no fireplace anywhere, and I wondered just how cold the library got during the winter.

"At least it isn't chilly up here compared to the studio," I muttered as I strolled toward the nearest bookshelves, quite determined to find as many good candidates as I could for that afternoon's entertainment. And before long, I was carefully climbing up the first ladder, eagerly peering at what felt like endless rows of weathered spines.

So many books! A good many of them were in foreign languages I couldn't read, and among those I could manage, I saw no real method as to the books' placement. My heart sank at the realization as I neared the very top shelf.

Novels, poetry books, volumes on history, geography, or even botany were simply thrown together following no clear thought besides the basic storage of these dusty collections. I had to sigh heavily and then descend the ladder. I simply had no idea how best to proceed with this task other than to just keep going with it.

Once I reached the middle row of books on the next set of shelves, I'd managed to overcome my dismay enough to actually enjoy perusing the spines and pulling a book out for a quick scan before deciding on it.

It took me a while, but at least I didn't have to complete the library's perimeter for my choices, but I eventually had an armful of books I could take back to my room. One of them would surely be something Rowena might find delightful enough to listen to.

In the course of gathering those books, I'd created a small pile on the chaise longue. I was in the middle of picking them up to carry off when a soft sound from the direction of the library door caught my attention. I looked up and found no one there.

How odd, I thought, because the sound I heard was of floorboards creaking under someone's weight as they walked stealthily toward the library and then hesitated at the threshold. Was one of the servants just there? I cradled the books against my chest and walked to the door, looking out and seeing no one else in either direction. Again, the upper hallway was deathly still though the calm outside was peppered with occasional birdsong.

I was sure there had been someone there. The sound was clear and, while quiet, had carried in the tomb-like silence of the upper floor. There had been someone tarrying just outside the door, perhaps looking in and watching me for a moment. But then I didn't hear any other sounds following it that would have indicated someone retreating hastily for fear of being caught.

In fact, the hallway was lengthy enough to prevent anyone's immediate disappearance around any corner since it only took me a handful of seconds to get to the door and look out after hearing the sounds. I took a deep breath as the hair up and down my arms stood, but it was all nonsense. I hurried off with my treasure and didn't dare a glance back.

Chapter 9

I presented myself to Rowena at the appointed time, a little disheartened when she said Cyrille was still in the studio hard at work on her portrait.

"We're nearly done with preliminary work. The gentleman does love to take his time," she said. She'd changed back to her usual gown, her manner apparently mirroring the subtler and more dignified fashion of a gentlewoman. Restrained, a little tired-looking, and again gazing around her with a dimmed and dreamy light in her pale eyes, she was back to how she was during my interview.

"He's—he's very talented," I offered after a brief's moment's awkward pause. "M. Boivin, I mean. He showed me all the watercolor studies he did of you, and I thought they were all marvelous."

Rowena nodded, a slight wrinkle forming between her brows as she drew a hand across them. "His talent runs deep. His father and grandfather were all commissioned to paint everything you see around you. Their family's remarkably blessed—though perhaps a bit erratic." She smiled at me then, the hard edge of her amusement back. "The grandfather painted me when I was still a young girl, but he only managed half a dozen before illness struck him, and the father took over the work. Majority of the paintings you see were done by him—M. Boivin's father, I mean."

And now it was Cyrille's turn. I glanced at one of two portraits on the wall of the drawing-room, marveling at the exquisite skill Cyrille's father had in his wielding of the brush. Erratic, though? Wasn't it typically an artistic temperament for the painter or sculptor to be erratic? I thought that was how genius was often expressed—in works of incomparable art.

"As for the sculptures, he'd had some help from his twin. Oh, yes, the father had a twin—also an artist. Equally as erratic, I'm afraid, but it seems that trait has bypassed the son. I'm pleased about that, you know. I want young M. Boivin to stick around longer than I, not succumb to the effects of a fevered brain." A wry little smile formed, and Rowena lightly tapped the side of her head with her finger.

I stood awkwardly before her, a book held against my chest, suddenly a little unnerved by her references to madness in Cyrille's family.

"Um—where would you like me to sit, ma'am?" I bleated.

"Oh, tsk! Didn't I tell you to call me Rowena?"

"Yes, ma'am, but—"

"Say it."

I swallowed. "Rowena."

She huffed, raising a brow at me. "That wasn't so hard now, was it?" I opened my mouth to respond, but she cut me off with a sharp flick of a wrist. "Sit by the window. No, not that window, Edgar, but the other one. Yes, that one. Is the window cushion comfortable enough for you?"

"Yes, it is," I stammered as I took my place where she ordered me. "There's plenty of light coming in here. I don't have to strain too hard to read the text."

"Excellent. The light suits you, my dear," she replied, settling comfortably against her loveseat's backrest. She seemed to drape herself over that piece of furniture as though she were posing for another portrait. She even threw an arm over the backrest in an attitude of indolence, her drawn features almost ghostly pale amid the dark and heavy furnishings. "From where I am, you look like you're crowned by some kind of ethereal light. There's a halo around you, almost. It's quite breathtaking."

I could only nod, unsure of how best to respond to her observations.

"That suit of yours won't do, though. Against the light, it looks too plain and shabby."

"Oh. I'm sorry, but I don't have expensive suits. Perhaps I should ask my father if—"

She flicked her wrist impatiently again. "Never mind that. Let's go on with the reading, my dear. What do you have in store for me?"

I fumbled the book open and nearly dropped it. "Poetry," I said, relieved by the change in subject and the chance to turn my attention to anything else but her. "It's Wordsworth—uh—I thought it would be fitting to read his rustic verses after seeing the painting M. Boivin was working on."

Rowena smiled again—a faint and almost sly kind of smile as she regarded me from the loveseat. "Call him Cyrille in my presence, young man. He specifically asked that you do him that honor."

I ducked my head and found the poem I'd marked for that afternoon's reading and proceeded, my voice faltering at first before finding its form and gaining the right amount of strength. For my first reading, I gave it all I had, weaving a poet's words with emotion and restraint, hoping I was able to convey a longing for idyllic days and melancholy for the forgotten poor. The poem itself was quite immersive, and I was soon lost in the words, the rhythm, the music, and especially the fleeting mental images formed by all.

Since Rowena didn't order me to rest or pause at any point, I carried on until my throat felt rather dry, and my voice began to falter a little. The distant sound of the clock chiming pulled me further out of the dream-state I seemed to be in, and I looked up to find her eyes closed.

"I'm not asleep," she murmured, and she opened her eyes and smiled. "Bravo, Edgar. You were marvelous. That was just the perfect poem for you."

"I'm afraid I'm not finished," I said. "My throat feels dry."

"Then we shall have tea. Mark your place, my dear, and we'll continue this evening."

I obeyed while she rose from her loveseat in one fluid move, apparently quite used to lounging upon it before company and certainly not at all looking self-conscious about her behavior. She lightly straightened her skirts and took in a deep breath while surveying her little drawing-room kingdom.

"We shall have tea in the temple," she declared. "It's at the farthest end of the flower field in the back. You wouldn't have seen it from the studio, but it's perfectly situated in a clearing in the wood. Go on and rest, Edgar. Tea will be served in an hour. That should give our M. Boivin ample time to finish his sketches."

Without another word, she swept out of the drawing-room, leaving me gaping after her with the book lying open on my lap.

The temple, as it turned out, was a folly, and it was most certainly situated in a perfect spot. Rowena boasted the clearing wasn't man-made which gave her even more incentive to erect a small stone temple. It was circular, with an elaborately designed domed roof held up by columns set upon the leaf-strewn platform. A small table and four chairs were already set up in the center, much to my surprise, but Rowena explained it was her custom to have the servants bring out these pieces during the spring months and then brought back inside when autumn held sway.

A dust cloth covered the setting, but it had been taken off for our purpose.

Cyrille joined us there, and tea turned into a most relaxing affair with artist and muse talking nearly non-stop about everything and nothing. I was simply too overwhelmed by everything that had taken place—and this on my first day here—to be a proper conversation partner and so contented myself with being a silent listener who'd respond in one or two words when prodded.

The rest of the day moved astonishingly rapidly, but I suppose it had everything to do with my newness to everything and perhaps inability to keep up with such a change. Indeed, I was so exhausted by the time dinner was called that I could only manage the soup and bread before excusing myself from the table.

"I shall see you in the morning, my dear," Rowena said when I pushed my chair back. She offered me one of her charming smiles again, her mood as high as her energy though I suspected her wildly shifting behavior was in part because of Cyrille's presence. "Breakfast is an idle affair, but Mrs. Quigg prefers that you be done with the meal no later than nine. Sleep in if you need the extra rest. I daresay it's been a most trying day for you."

"It's quite a change from what I'm used to," I replied, blushing, my gaze flicking over to Cyrille who was once again watching me keenly from his chair. "I promise to be an early riser tomorrow morning."

Rowena inclined her head in a stately nod. "Very good, my dear. Good night."

"Good night, ma'am." I caught myself and stammered, "Good night, Rowena."

She chuckled and shook her head, waved me away, and was almost immediately drawn back into conversation with Cyrille. I spared him one final glance, marveling in his beauty, and bade him good night as well before all but scampering off like a guilty schoolboy after claiming a candle lamp to light my way around.

I met Mrs. Quigg upstairs, who'd apparently just prepared my bedroom for the night.

"You have a new ewer of water and fresh towels," she said with a pleasant smile. I readily responded to her easy and friendly manner—a far cry from the more strained air I felt around Rowena or, sadly, Cyrille. "Have you had a good first day, Mr. Cushing?"

"Very good, thank you, Mrs. Quigg. It's just a lot to absorb in such a short amount of time," I said with a self-deprecating chuckle and a shrug. "Does, uh, Mrs. Fairclough have a set schedule she follows every day?"

"Not really, no, unless she's sitting for another one of her portraits. I'm afraid her health's quite fragile, and that dictates all activity for the day."

"Of course. I quite understand. Um—she has a lot of them here—portraits, I mean."

"Nothing less would do, Mr. Cushing." Mrs. Quigg's tone spoke of a motherly fondness and protectiveness toward her mistress, and I immediately shut down any more wry observations about the house's oddities. "You'll find my lady quite the bold, independent spirit. What she says, goes, and she expects nothing less than obedience and a not impossibly high standard in behavior around here."

I nodded. "Yes, ma'am."

Mrs. Quigg eyed me speculatively for a second or two. "She's excessively fond of you, I see. Oh, don't look so startled, young man. Consider that high praise coming from such a lady."

"She expects me to address her by her name."

"Then you should do so. I know it's highly unusual, but she's not the sort to be tested if you get my meaning. Simply do as you're told, and you'll be compensated handsomely and treated like one of the family." She nodded in the direction of the stairs. "Have you managed to take a tour around the house yet? Or the grounds?" At my negative, she said, "You'll have plenty of time now. If you wish to send a letter out to your father, just hand it over to me, and I'll have Mr. Grieve take it to town when he comes around for our supplies."

"Thank you, ma'am."

"Oh, you charming thing. Good night, Mr. Cushing." Mrs. Quigg grinned broadly and then moved off, humming softly to herself.

The walk to my room, which stood at the far end of the hallway, left me a little unnerved because no candle was lit anywhere along the way. Only my candle lamp aided me, and the silent stone nymphs made me feel as though eyes watched me from the shadows. Now and then a statue's outstretched hand made me slow my walk and consider it, wondering if it had just moved in an effort to touch me.

The awful silence of the upper floor hallway didn't help matters, either. I knew Rowena's bedroom was on the opposite wing though I didn't know where the guest bedroom was. I suspected it was somewhere on my side, but I never bothered to ask. Everything was simply moving too quickly for me to remember things.

I entered my bedroom and was relieved to find a fully lit candelabrum standing proudly on a small table between the bed and the washstand. It helped chase the deeper shadows away given the relatively cluttered nature of my bedroom and its large and heavy pieces of furniture. The books I carried off from the library sat where I left them on my bed, and I eagerly changed, washed myself again to clear my head and relax me. Once I'd put on my nightshirt, folded my clothes and set them aside along with the early pile I'd made, I crawled under the heavy blankets with a book.

"Ouch!" I cried when my backside pressed against something hard.

I fumbled around and pulled out the offending object and saw that it was the wooden toy soldier I'd discovered earlier. I stared at it in surprise. Didn't I put it inside my coat pocket? I thought I did, and in fact I'd completely forgotten about the toy with all the things I had to do. Even during those brief restful interludes, I'd spent the time reading the same book of poetry I used for Rowena's afternoon entertainment.

"Well—I'll have to sort you out tomorrow, then," I said to the little soldier before setting it down beside the candelabrum. "In the meantime, stay there."

As I tried to settle back down in bed, my gaze strayed to the pile of books I'd moved from my bed, and I noticed something sticking out of one of them. A piece of heavy paper, I thought as I picked u the volume, and I carefully pulled it out.

It was a torn page of something, and there was my face, looking back at me with a small, almost puzzled smile curving my mouth. The angle of the portrait told me it was captured from above, so that I was looking up—quite likely while elbow-deep in grass and flowers. It was a watercolor study of me with Cyrille's initials near the bottom.

Chapter 10

The rain arrived with the dawn—a sudden and rather startling event given the pleasant sunniness of the previous day. I awoke to a dimmed and moody house, fully refreshed from yesterday's adventures and loving the steady sound of rainfall outside my windows. After washing thoroughly and fussing over my uncooperative hair yet again, I headed downstairs.

I didn't expect to be sent out to gather more flowers for Rowena though I did hope she wouldn't insist upon a rain jacket or something to get her way.

Other than the occasional voice of a servant from some unknown part of the house, all was silent as I went straight for the dining-room. I stuffed my hands in my pockets without thought and felt the toy soldier in one. I couldn't remember putting it back in my pocket after finding it in my bed last night. Then again, I couldn't remember taking it out of my pocket at any time yesterday, either.

"Well, you're here now," I said to the sad little weathered toy and then dropped it back in my pocket.

I admit to being dismayed at my forgetfulness regardless of the sudden and drastic change in my circumstances. Surely I wouldn't be so easily influenced by my environment to the point where I could barely function without being constantly reminded or surprised by something I couldn't recall doing. At eighteen, surely I could adapt far better than this!

A hectic day like yesterday wouldn't have made me forget so easily, would it? I sighed and entered the dining-room to find no one there. The sideboard was still quite piled high with covered dishes, and I greedily helped myself to breakfast.

Mrs. Quigg appeared just when I was finishing off my first serving of breakfast to inspect my progress. Apparently she found it much to her satisfaction judging from the pleased little smile and slight nod she gave me.

"I hope you had a restful night in your new room," she said at length, taking her place by the sideboard and resting her hands over her voluminous skirts. "I know it's quite different from what you're used to, but we did try to make it as comfortable and welcoming as possible."

"I had a very good night, thank you. Oh—Mrs. Quigg, I think someone left this behind while cleaning the room." I stood up and walked toward her, holding up the toy soldier. "I found it on my bed sometime after I unpacked. Perhaps one of the servants forgot. Does any of them have a little boy?"

Mrs. Quigg eyed the wooden toy in her hand and then shrugged. "I'll ask around. None of the maids are married, but this could be a little brother's or nephew's. Thank you, Mr. Cushing."

Another word of encouragement from her and I was helping myself to yet another plate. Mrs. Quigg watched me in silence for another moment before moving away to stoke the fire in another part of the dining-room.

"Mrs. Fairclough is expecting you in her study after breakfast—no later than ten, she says."

"Of course. Should I be needing the book I read to her yesterday?"

Mrs. Quigg appeared to consider her answer while prodding the fire with a poker. "I don't think so. If she requests your presence in her study, it's likely for something secretarial."

I sat back down with my newly refilled plate and glanced at Mrs. Quigg's crouched figure before the fire. She'd already set the poker aside, and just as she was about to stand up, she flung something small into the blaze. To my amazement it was the toy soldier—or at least I was convinced of it since it was the only thing she was surely holding then.

I frowned at her back as she rose but immediately looked back down at my plate when she turned to face me.

"Enjoy your breakfast, Mr. Cushing," she said as cheerfully as ever, and I glanced up with as innocent as smile as I could manage.

"Thank you, Mrs. Quigg. This is very good."

"I should hope so, young man. Nothing but the very best for my mistress's table."

She left me blinking at her retreating figure before turning my attention back to the fire. For one mad moment, I had half a mind to run to the fire and see if I could save the toy soldier, but reason prevailed. The fire was a sizable blaze, and something as small and fragile-looking as the soldier wouldn't have survived more than five seconds in there. I finished my breakfast lost in thought though in time the steady and gentle patter of the rain outside eased my mind, and that brief yet strange moment was soon forgotten in favor of other, more pleasing things.

Like Cyrille, for instance. I didn't hear him at all, let alone glimpse him anywhere as I went down to breakfast. Perhaps he was back in the studio working some more on Rowena's portrait. Was it too bold for me to pay him a visit in his workshop? I thought to find out when I repaired to the studio immediately after breakfast.

In the gloom of a gray day, the house's interior hid in half-formed shadows, and stone nymphs standing in silent guardianship of Rowena's castle looked more like watchful ghosts peering out from their secret places. I tried not to look at them as I walked past. I'm not ashamed to admit that I was quite relieved at the generous spaciousness of the house's passageways. In the daytime hours, at least I was fully aware of it. Night brought about it a wholly different perspective, of course, and moving about with nothing more than a candle lamp to help me see my way didn't aid matters at all.

Before long I was peering inside the door to the studio, sweeping my gaze around and finding no signs of Cyrille anywhere. The easel upon which had sat the canvas yesterday was now empty. Nothing else appeared to have changed overnight, the canvases in various states of completion (if at all in most cases) were as I remembered them, all leaning against each other and the walls. The studio still looked as disarrayed as it did yesterday, but with Cyrille not there, I thought to leave his sanctuary alone.

A sudden blast of chill air blew against me, and I shrank back with a shudder.

Ah! Aaahh!

I froze at the door and held my breath as I waited. Did someone just whisper something? Frowning, I peered inside again, this time taking a step across the threshold without releasing my hold on the door.

"Is anyone in here?" I called out. Nothing but a hollow silence answered. "Good morning! Is anyone in here?"

Again, nothing. I sighed and withdrew, pulling the door shut as I stepped back out into the hallway. What an idiotic thing to do, I chided myself as I walked off. There was no place for anyone to hide in the studio unless they were the size of a cat, and they were thin and flat enough to squeeze into crevices or gaps in the sideboards where Cyrille kept his tools, rags, paints, and other things.

The studio being so cold all the time surely meant some unfortunate cracks in the walls or windows somewhere. There was also that door that directly led people out to the rear part of the flower field. Perhaps there was a gap somewhere in the doorframe or the door itself that allowed an abnormal amount of cold air to enter the studio.

Another maid stepped out into the hallway, and I was obliged to ask for directions to the study. The room was upstairs, as it happened, in the same wing as Rowena's bedroom. I immediately went up the stairs, my mind still on the curious iciness of the studio. How awful it must be for poor Cyrille to keep working under such conditions. How could he manage to spend so many hours in that cold room? Was he used to it now, or was he simply obliged to hold his tongue about it since complaints would surely lead to a dismissal?

"Wait a moment," I muttered, pausing in my tracks halfway up the grand staircase as I chased after a thought. "It wasn't at all cold yesterday. Within doors and without, even, including my bedroom. Yet the studio was still too chilly even with the rear door and windows open the whole time Cyrille was there."

It took me another moment to shake myself impatiently. Such nonsense! Such stupid ideas! What on earth was I doing? I bit back an angry growl and walked on resolutely.

Rowena was already in her study when I knocked and entered. Dressed as impeccably as always, she nevertheless looked quite wan and wilting, her pale eyes looking as though they barely saw anything around her. Distraction was in her air again as she spoke tentatively. Yesterday's energy and confidence seemed to have been nothing more than illusion as I wordlessly took my place behind a small writing-desk as commanded.

"You'll be writing a letter for me," she said after a moment's clumsy pause between us. She glanced around her, a slight frown creasing her brows, and she appeared to cock her head a little as though listening for something. In another second, she was mentally back in the room with me. "Forgive me," she stammered with a lifeless chuckle as she paced ever so slowly before the writing-desk. "I wasn't feeling well when I woke up this morning."

"Oh. Should I ask for a doctor?"

Rowena waved a hand distractedly. "No need. Thank you, my dear. I'll be all right soon enough."

"Well—"

"Let's get on with the letter, shall we?" She nodded at me and smiled in a way that felt apologetic, and I relaxed in my chair. "Now this is for the frame maker—a Signor Arcangelo Di Pasqua of Pienza. He's responsible for a third of the frames you see on the walls."

Instinctively I looked at a painting hanging just to my right. It was a portrait of Rowena offering a knight in gold armor a blood-red rose. I nodded in appreciation at the gorgeously designed frame around it.

"It's sublime, isn't it, Edgar? I try to cast a wide net in my search for frame makers. Nothing less than the best craftsman will do my art any justice," Rowena said dreamily. "I'd like to commission the good signore for another series of frames. Last night M. Boivin and I discussed the new collection I'm paying him handsomely for, and only Signor Di Pasqua's extraordinary skill in capturing my wishes will elevate this collection further."

I found a clean sheet of paper in the drawer and prepared the pen and ink as I listened to her extol her frame maker's virtues. Then she fell silent, and I waited with pen in hand.

"Have you ever had a portrait of yourself made, my dear?"

I looked up to find her observing me closely and keenly. There seemed to be a strange, wild light in her eyes as though she'd just spotted something quite special in what she was staring at. Her faded energy had been revitalized, and there was an air of almost stupefied wonder in her as she pinned me down with her gaze.

"No, I haven't. I'm afraid Papa couldn't really afford anything so special." I almost said "frivolous" because talent aside, Rowena's artists had been kept busy filling the walls with expensive and frivolous things. I thought her paintings were something like follies such as the stone temple in the wood.

"But such a waste—to have this beauty ignored and not celebrated? Not immortalized?"

"I really don't think I'm handsome enough for art," I replied, blushing. Well, I suppose I looked good enough to stir some fevered imaginings among older students when I was in school, but that was neither here nor there as far as I was concerned.

And then I suddenly remembered Cyrille's unexpected gift of the watercolor study, and I held my tongue.

Rowena waved my doubts away with her usual wrist-flick as I now called it. "No matter. Let's carry on. I do tarry too much sometimes when—especially when I'm not feeling too well, I'm afraid. But no talk about doctors, Edgar. Let's finish this, and I'll have Mrs. Quigg bring me something to clear my head."

The next moment was spent writing an offer of a commission in a language and manner that was elegance and restraint as befitting a noblewoman. Nothing I wrote betrayed the strangely depleted but proud lady pacing before the desk, and even more curious was the fact that the longer she expressed her wishes and laid out in great detail the design she hoped to see, the more energized she became.

It was as if her busy imagination, weaving a pattern from nothing, was feeding her body as well. Not with anything substantial on which she could find sufficient purchase and hoist her weary self up with, but with vague and airy hope that allowed her to soar if only in her head. But if that was the only thing that could give her the fire she seemed to need, who was I to object to whatever castles in the air she was now seeing?

The letter ran two full pages long because she spared no details, and when I was obliged to stop and rest my tired wrist, she swept up to me to review the letter, approve everything with a brilliant smile, and then thank me with a firm shake of a hand.

Chapter 11

The letter I wrote to Signor Di Pasqua spurred me into writing one of reassurance to Papa. With Rowena's permission, I took some of the paper from the writing-desk and was also supplied with a pen and an ink bottle.

"Go on and take those with you. I can always buy a new set," she said while I gratefully gathered my treasure, dismissing me with a wan smile that made her look all the more alarming as I was convinced she was feeling more ill than she let on.

The earlier fire when she dictated her letter was well and fully gone by now, and all that was left was a wisp of a woman—a phantom that barely made a sound with every movement. And I was afraid that she'd simply fade until she vanished completely the longer she stayed.

Unfortunately my bedroom didn't have a proper surface on which to write, and it was also Rowena's suggestion to make full use of the library instead. Be creative with its contents, in fact.

"There are so many monstrously sized atlases in that room you can use as a writing surface," she added before withdrawing to her room for further rest. I waited until she was back in her bedroom before moving on, alarm easing into simple concern for her well-being and feeling quite at a loss.

Mrs. Quigg seemed to have a finely tuned instinct of some kind when it came to her beloved mistress because I'd barely made it to the upper floor landing when she appeared, mouth set in a tight line, her gaze steely with intent. She even barely acknowledged me with a nod.

"Is she going to be all right?" I asked once she drew near. "I can run for the doctor if you tell me where to go. The rain won't bother me, I swear."

"No, no—there's no need for that," she replied hurriedly as she sailed past. "She's always out of sorts or just fading like this when Mr. Boivin leaves. Now off with you, young man. You may be spending the rest of the day alone, I'm afraid, but if you need anything, I'll be downstairs. Pray don't bother the other servants. Come to me directly, all right?"

"Yes, ma'am."

Mrs. Quigg didn't seem to hear me and was soon gone, melting into the deeper shadows of the hallway before completely vanishing inside Rowena's bedroom.

I sagged a little, my spirits sinking. Cyrille was gone? I'd hoped to spend a little more time with him that day, but I suppose one couldn't get everything worth having.

The library was going to be my favorite retreat, I thought on my entry. Books had always offered me a special sort of comfort, and being so fully surrounded by tall shelves that required a ladder to reach felt like heaven. I paused at the doorway and even took a deep breath, committing to memory the smell of aging paper, leather, and ink, which seemed to permeate everything in that magnificent room. Even the more modern furnishings and elaborate decorations couldn't hide what I'd call the primeval nature of old books.

My thoughts strayed to the now absent Cyrille, and the weight of loneliness began to press down on me. I wished he stayed so I could have someone else to talk to, but I understood his position entirely. Unless he was a resident artist whose lodging was also a part of his contract with Rowena, he had no reason to stay in Bridewater House indefinitely.

I thought about what Mrs. Quigg had also said about Cyrille elevating Rowena's moods, and I had to smile ruefully. That man truly had a magical way of affecting others, and with any luck, this new collection he'd just been commissioned to do would mean a more consistent appearance hereabouts.

I kept the door to the hallway open to allow what little light there was on such a rainy day to pour inside somehow. I also took care to light the candelabra, which might be a touch dramatic on my part, but something had urged me to keep the room as well-lit as possible despite the time of the day. The incident involving the creaking floorboards outside the library just a day ago had returned, and I didn't feel so easy in my mind at the reminder.

After another moment spent searching, I found one of those atlases Rowena had mentioned and was soon lost in writing a fairly brief letter on the chaise with the heavy, oversized volume on my lap. I wrote about my adventures so far, but I took care not to say anything about the strangeness of Bridewater House. I didn't want to alarm my father, of course, but then again, there really wasn't any reason for the place to cause *any* concern in anyone. The idiosyncrasies certainly gave the entire place a very unusual and unique flavor, in a manner of speaking, but that was all.

By the time I was done with my letter, I'd filled up a page and a half and hoped that was enough to set Papa's mind to rest on my account. I then placed the letter aside, the sheets lying side by side in order to let the ink dry, and before long I was again climbing one of the ladders and scouring bookshelves I'd never gotten around to exploring the previous day.

I still had a book in my room that I hadn't finished, but the rain had made me lethargic and feeling too lazy to fetch it. I thought then to stick around the library and thought to pass the time with another volume.

I stretched out on the longue chaise, propping myself up with a couple of the plump pillows lying around, and I was soon reading.

Now and then I'd pause and hold my breath, straining my ears to listen closely. As usual, the upper hallway outside the library was deathly silent though this time the steady pattering of the rain outside lent the area a relatively soothing atmosphere.

Whether or not it was pure fancy, memory, or simply the normal sounds of an old house when left alone, there were the occasional creaks and groans that drew me away from the book. They were few and far between, and they were also tentatively soft that I didn't feel the same unease the way I did yesterday.

What did startle me was the distant and vague feeling of somehow being watched. Once or twice I set my book down and looked directly at the open door but saw no one there. I even stood up and walked out, turning around and making sure I was, indeed, alone there. Bridewater House might as well be a crypt given the way an absolute silence bore down on it from room to room, especially on the upper floor.

I eventually fell asleep on the longue, lulled by the rain, the book, and the pressing silence around me. I think I dreamt of Cyrille, but I couldn't be too sure. I did drift off with a soft warmth in my chest as I recalled the lovely watercolor study he'd done. It was now safely tucked away with my clothes, and I hoped to keep it forever.

I didn't know how long I slept, but it was clearly a long enough time for the candles to gutter and the skies outside to darken further. I woke up to the near darkness in the library as well as the distinct feeling of someone else loitering in the room with me though I could neither see nor hear any movement. Caught in that state between full consciousness and sleep, my senses seemed to be both heightened and deadened with my sleep-addled brain growing more and more aware of the unseen presence.

I couldn't speak as I struggled against the effects of sleep, but the deepening conviction of a second person in the library kept me hovering in a state of confusion and fear.

The book I was reading had fallen off and was now somewhere on the floor next to the chaise. I tried to turn my attention to that in a fumbling effort at distraction when the sounds—no, the *certainty*—of soft, quiet movement inside the library did away with whatever sleepy lethargy still kept a hold on me. There *was* someone else there, walking and making as little noise as possible as though determined not to wake me.

The darkness in the library was such that I could still make out shapes, but try as I might, I could see nothing even vaguely resembling a human figure creeping about. I lay sprawled on the chaise, unable to move, confusion and fear turning completely into a crippling terror as I tried to follow the movements with as many of my senses as I could.

There were soft footsteps and yet there weren't. Shadows played cruel tricks on one's perceptions as sounds seemed to be both real and yet primarily sensed in the deepest corner of my mind. And I sensed those footsteps nearing me. My breaths turned shallow and rapid, my eyes widening as they tried and failed to catch the source of the movements, and my limbs stayed frozen in place.

The *feeling* of the footsteps stopped near the chaise.

Then a small, icy hand took one of mine in a shy hold.

I still saw no one else in the room with me. I still heard nothing that convinced me the hand clutching mine belonged to someone living.

My tongue had fused itself somehow in my mouth, my throat turning to stone. Terror as I'd never known before overcame me, but I couldn't move a muscle if my life depended upon it. I simply lay on the chaise, paralyzed with unbearable horror, while an unseen child held my hand. I didn't know how long I stayed in that position, but it felt like a dreadful eternity with no other sounds but the increasingly heavy rain outside keeping up with the loud and ragged breaths being torn out of me.

Then the distant footsteps of someone walking down the passageway caught my attention, and when I at first wondered if those were yet another nightmarish fancy, the steady pace and the increasing loudness told me there was someone coming my way. And just as the realization dawned, the small, icy hand in mine vanished.

A light appeared in the doorway, and Mrs. Quigg's most welcome figure followed.

"Why, Mr. Cushing," she cried. "I was about to cover you with a blanket and let you continue sleeping there."

I saw then that she was holding a folded blanket and a candle lamp, and with my heart still thundering and my breaths coming out in terrified, rapid bursts, I forced myself to sit up while rubbing my hands together. The memory of that awful moment lingered, and I fought against the terror that left my hair standing on end and my voice nearly useless.

I think I made some sort of noncommittal sound in my throat in answer—indeed, I could do nothing more for the time being. And I sought comfort in the sight of Mrs. Quigg going about her task of tidying up the library with the help of nothing more than her candle lamp.

"What time is it?" I managed to croak.

"Just past noon. I'm afraid you missed lunch, but there's still food downstairs," she replied cheerfully. "Mrs. Fairclough took her meal in her room, and she might be coming out for tea. Depends on how well she feels by then, of course, but you've got the rest of the day quite free."

I nodded as I fumbled for my letter and barely managed to keep them from being ruined by my still-trembling hands. My terror melted away the longer Mrs. Quigg stayed with me, and I suspected she refused to leave the room until I took myself back downstairs for lunch. And I was very, very grateful for her constant hovering.

She led me out of the library and distracted me further with constant chatter about the wretched weather and the wretched silence that always followed whenever Rowena all but locked herself away in her room.

"I must say I'm mightily glad you're here with us now," she said as we walked down the stairs. "It's been so lonely with no one else keeping poor Mrs. Fairclough company—even as a secretary or assistant. Mr. Boivin can only stay so long and so often, obviously, so having a young gentleman like yourself really eases the heavy silence around here."

She shuddered almost dramatically.

"It's like living in a crypt sometimes, but don't tell Mrs. Fairclough that. She doesn't mind the silence and the solitude, but I know she desperately needs company, and the library can only do so much for her."

By the time we reached the ground floor landing, I was feeling very much like myself again, and a part of me started to throw doubt upon that dreadful moment in the library. The newness of my situation, the strangeness of Bridewater House, my inexperience in being around strangers day in and day out, and the unexpected turn of the weather...

Surely all of those could play endless, awful tricks on one's mind, especially when they happened to be emerging from an unexpected nap. I clutched my letter against my chest as though it were some kind of childish talisman against unknown forces. My father didn't need to know this, I reminded myself. There was no need to make him panic over an overactive imagination.

All the way to the dining-room I chided myself until I couldn't stand to listen to my mental voice any longer. At least the food that Mrs. Quigg had prepared for lunch smelled good enough to tear my attention back to the missed meal, and the bright fire dancing merrily across the room cheered me up even more.

As I ate and felt my strength and spirits restore themselves, I swore to do much better, keep my head and not be such an utter coward. And Mrs. Quigg, bless her, seemed to have understood my dilemma last night because she placed a number of lit candles along the passageway leading to my bedroom later that evening, much to my relief, though I still took care to bring my candle lamp with me.

Chapter 12

The heavy rains persisted for two more days, and so did the awful gloom shrouding the house. Rowena herself continued to look ill and haggard though she at least put up a cheerful enough front when I kept her company. Her manner was just as open but commanding, alternately distracted and brusque, gently encouraging and acerbically critical.

With Cyrille still absent, a sullen silence lingered, one that I didn't have the wit to fight. Indeed, I couldn't help but be cowed by the deadening nothingness shadowing me at every turn and, to my great shame, depended upon my ill employer for strength. Not that Rowena noticed, judging from her readiness to engage me in conversation or command me to do this or that as though she were soaring in perfect health. At least I wasn't ordered back to the library for more books because I seemed to have stumbled upon a favorite volume of hers, and I carried on with my reading of Wordsworth's poetry according to her wishes.

Ah, yes, her wishes.

The second day of steady rain found me being told to sit on the rug before the fire in such a way as to appear quite relaxed and indolent. Rowena ordered me to move the ottoman close, and against it I was to lean with one arm resting on its surface while I read with the open book on the floor.

"Drape" would be a much more apt description, I think.

And in the meantime, Rowena took to a recamier that hadn't been there before, laying herself on it so that she, too, was half-draped lazily over the scrolled arm closest to me. Together we made quite the picture of a pair of relations enjoying a quiet and cozy moment before the fire. I reckoned if Cyrille were present, he'd have been able to paint us both, and I wouldn't be able to recognize myself in the final work.

It was the sort of image best suited for illustrating with sure pencil-strokes, not words on paper. I daresay I was convinced no amount of writing or struggling with vocabulary would suffice in properly conveying the strange tableau we must have presented. Rowena listened with her eyes closed and her drawn face soft and peaceful, her chin resting on her bent and crossed arms.

Around us nothing but my quietly modulated voice, the soft crackling of the fire nearby, and the gentle pattering of the rain outside could be heard. It was, in all honesty, the sort of environment I'd consider to be perfect for such an activity on such a day.

Yet a vague and subtle unease wove itself into my head, an insistent spectral prodding that made me look upon my reading hour with doubt though there was nothing about it that was in any way threatening. Again I forced myself to slow my racing thoughts down later that day and revisit the moment while the memory was still very fresh. And no matter what I did, no matter how many times I turned things over in my mind, I still came up quite short of an answer. Yes, Rowena and I would have made a most peculiar scene as though we were acting out an idyllic moment in a story or book, but that was about it.

She wasn't cross, she didn't criticize me at all, and she even appeared to be lost in a most pleasant dream the whole time she listened to me. Perhaps my reading of the poem loosened old memories that gave her much happiness. Beloved scraps of time from her childhood or youth? I wouldn't be surprised if such were the case. Indeed, I'd look up now and then in the course of my reading to ensure she was still listening, and I'd see a tender smile lighting up her wan features. Not once did she interrupt me, and my voice lasted much longer since Rowena also took care to have a glass of water nearby specifically for me.

But that unease stuck with me, and the hour ended with me all the more baffled by the unfounded worry. I even fought off the idea—unbidden and un-wanted—of the moment being decidedly unnatural and purposefully designed for some dark purpose. What a thought! Anyone would easily consider me a most annoying child with no control over his wretched imagination.

"Are you restless, my dear?" Rowena asked me over lunch—a decidedly muted affair with her commandeering the conversation with bits of stories she'd loved as a girl through her collection of books and art.

"I—I'm sorry. I don't know what to do with myself when it's pouring out-side like this for more than a day," I replied with a sheepish little smile. Rowena's pastoral likeness eyed me from a nearby frame, her gaze blazing with playful en-ergy.

"I know you're not of an artistic bent, but you're welcome to pass the time practicing a sketch or two," she said with a light jerk of her head in the direc-tion of the dining-room doors. "The studio houses several unused sketchbooks I've purchased for my artist's pleasure. There are also plenty of pencils to use, all properly sharpened. Take one of each and turn to them when reading for your own pleasure no longer engages you."

I nodded and thanked her, and the conversation died completely. I wondered how Papa was doing and hoped to request a weekend at home once I was settled in and comfortable in my new lodgings. It would be shabby to plead for two days off together after just a week or even a fortnight at my new job. I told myself to wait till after a month at the very least, but in the meantime, I could always write home every week.

I hadn't received a letter from my father yet, but I didn't expect him to write back so soon, let alone write back at all. As much as I'd liked to have read a brief missive from Papa, I knew better than to encourage him and even said so in my first letter home.

I went to the studio almost immediately after lunch. The door stood open, much to my surprise, since I knew Cyrille wasn't there that day. I peered inside and saw no one inside and so assumed it had been nothing more than a servant who'd cleaned and perhaps forgotten to ensure that the door was fully closed upon leaving.

It didn't take me long to find the sketchbooks. A good number of them were stored in one of the sideboards' drawers, and among them were at least a dozen pencils just strewn across the haphazardly piled books. I quickly snatched a pencil and a sketchbook, shivering a little in the cold and startled at the soft puff of cloud that blew out of my mouth when I exhaled. I turned around, frowning, when awareness of just how drastically chilly it was in the studio overcame me—chillier than ever, I mean.

I took that moment to search for possible openings or improperly sealed or shut windows, but while I saw nothing, I really couldn't say I knew exactly what to look for. But I did know a badly ventilated room if I were in one and so resolved to tell Rowena my observations.

I shut the studio door behind me, making sure to listen to the soft snick of the latch. The hinges creaked as well, but it seemed that all door hinges in Bridewater House creaked or groaned when moving. I walked away for several feet before stopping, my senses suddenly on alert. All was silent in the hallway, but I glanced back all the same and stared in surprise at the sight of the studio door standing wide open.

"A faulty latch, I'm sure," I muttered with a sigh as I walked back to the studio and shut the door again. I tested it a couple of times, in fact, opening and closing twice, each time jiggling the doorknob and ensuring the door stayed firmly shut and feeling satisfied with it.

Another item of concern that needed to be discussed with Rowena, I thought, walking down the hallway again. When I reached the far corner, I looked back again and found the door standing ajar once more. But how? I didn't hear a single creak both times that thing swung open! I swallowed, my feet suddenly rooted, but this time I heeded the soft voice in my head urging me to move immediately. My steps back to the main part of the house were hurried and my progress almost blind.

"Mrs. Quigg!" I cried when I clapped eyes on her as she was ascending the stairs. "May I ask you something?"

She paused midway, blinking in surprise, but smiled indulgently at me. "Of course, dear. What is it?"

"Um..." The words died, and I found myself reluctant to say a word all of a sudden. I didn't know what held me back then, but it was real enough and compelling enough to force obedience.

"Yes?" she prodded. A baffled smile took over as she waited for me to say something.

"Uh—the studio? I—I think there's something wrong with the door." When Mrs. Quigg tilted her head inquiringly, the puzzled look on her face still there, I stammered, "It—it won't stay shut."

"The studio door? Oh, well, that shouldn't come as a surprise. Haven't you been told? It's the oldest room in the house and was part of the original structure before great parts of it fell into ruin from neglect. Mrs. Fairclough did well in keeping that room intact, getting the rest of the old house demolished, and this new one built in its place. Or at least the rest of the house was built around the studio, anyway, if you get my meaning."

"So that's why the door's faulty? I found it open when I went there, and I did close it behind me and even tested the latch, but it opened itself anyway when my back was turned. And—and it did so twice within a minute or something."

Mrs. Quigg snickered. "Don't let that alarm you, my dear, as that sort of thing's happened before. I'm so used to living in such a house that what's strange to others are terribly mundane to me."

"The room itself is also much colder than the rest of the house, I've noticed."

Mrs. Quigg nodded. "Yes, it's always been colder, but Mrs. Fairclough prefers to keep things as they are, especially that room. It holds a very special place in her heart, you know." She paused and considered. "In fact, one could say the studio's the heart of the house given what it contains. And as for the door, I'll have someone look at it. I do hope you're not entertaining any farfetched ideas about that room. Old houses will have their way."

I considered what I'd heard. Bridewater House was designed with peculiarities in mind, and preserving a relic from the past—and perhaps the last connection she had with her bloodline—made some sense. A melancholy connection, perhaps, considering the studio's state of perpetual irregularity and lack of a cohesive link to the rest of the house.

All the same, I couldn't explain the incident with the wooden toy soldier and even Mrs. Quigg's final destruction of it. The library now left me a little cautious though I couldn't prove or disprove the reality of my experience with an unseen companion even if the touch of a little hand in mine felt real enough. I sought reassurance from the more plausible explanation of a barely conscious mind and the darkness of the room all playing wicked tricks on my imagination.

"Is that a sketchbook I see?" Mrs. Quigg asked, her cheerful voice breaking through my thoughts.

"It is. I'd like to pass the time doing something else but read when it's raining so hard like this."

"Poor dear. If it's any comfort, we expect Mr. Boivin to be back soon enough. The rains might be keeping him away for now, but he has connections who can lend him a more proper conveyance in terrible weather. His work's not done as far as I know."

"Yes, ma'am."

"By the bye, have you any letters you wish to send home?"

"No, ma'am. I wrote home just a couple of days ago. Does Rowena wish for another business letter?"

"She does, but she'll tell you herself since I don't know if it's later or tomorrow. For now, enjoy a bit of time to yourself, dear. I know it's quite dull hereabouts when the weather's forcing you indoors, and you've no one else your age to talk to." Mrs. Quigg gently patted my arm and let me pass her.

Since I didn't hear her footsteps following me up the rest of the stairs, I wondered if she stood and watched me the whole time. I tried not to think too much about it, the relief I felt when I heard about the studio easing any lingering discomfort or doubts I had earlier.

The rains had eased a little by then, the earlier heavy and relentless barrage turning into the more favorable quiet and steady patter. The clouds also lifted a little, allowing more light through, and it was gratifying being able to sit by the window for a bit of reading, feeling snug and cozy with a large blanket wrapped around me and fully covering my legs and feet.

I kept the watercolor sketch Cyrille had done of me close by, occasionally glancing at it and feeling my heart skip in pleasure. Was this how he saw me, or was he simply being an artist, flattering his subject?

Reading eventually gave way for a need for rest, and I sleepily moved from armchair to bed, shedding the blanket along the way and crawling under the thick blankets. Whether or not it was proper for me to sleep in the middle of the day, I couldn't tell, but I felt like I desperately needed it and simply had no will to fight the pull.

And that pull was awfully powerful, dragging me through that plane of sleep-and-yet-not. My imagination was once again under such a potent influence, prey to every idea and image that came from every possible source. Indeed, just as I was sinking into oblivion, I half-dreamt of someone climbing into bed with me, tentatively pushing their way under the blankets as well and settling down in contented rest beside me. I heard no other sound—no footsteps, no rustling bedclothes, no breathing. I sensed it, though, as one usually did when one drifted off to sleep, the feeble awareness of someone else in bed with me vying for attention with the knowledge that my bedroom was just as chilly as the studio.

Chapter 13

Rowena dictated another letter over tea. It was another business letter to be sent to a Mr. Christophorus Schuyler, an artist from Rotterdam who provided richly detailed illustrations for many of the novels she owned. This time she was inquiring after possible commissions for another set of books she'd set her heart on—books so beautifully written, she said, but so shabbily devoid of proper images that could have enhanced such magical stories.

"It's simply too bad these books are already printed. I'll have to commission a set of illustrations for them though perhaps bound separately as companion volumes to the books I possess. It's not a perfect solution, but the illustrated volumes will have to be something like novelty collectible books, I suppose," she said with a regretful sigh. "Now let me read what you've written."

After another moment, she declared herself very satisfied, commended me for my clarity and "exquisite penmanship", and then told me to post the letter after breakfast the following morning. Someone from town was to come by, and it would be my duty to wait for him at the end of the drive just where it met the main road. He wasn't expected to come into the drive, so all posts had to be handed over to him as he passed.

"I've just had Mrs. Quigg bring up the cloak you're to wear. It's a quick errand, to be sure, but after the rains we've had, I expect the day to be dry tomorrow but also to start off with some fog. It's been my observation, you see. I do take the weather rather seriously though it might seem a strange habit of mine." She smiled vaguely, her gaze drifting toward the windows and the darkness outside. The rain had eased further by then to a barely heard taps against the glass. "One can't help it when one lives as I do."

"A cloak? I have a thick coat I can use. It's kept me warm and dry before."

"You'll wear the cloak I sent up to your room, my dear. Now good night."

I withdrew from Rowena's study and returned to my bedroom. The cloak was, indeed, there, neatly laid out on the bed, and I couldn't help but blink. It was a curious piece of clothing, that was for sure, but in the sense that it was very much something like a relic of ages long past. Made of a very heavy and thick black material—wool, I think—it was also lined with such fine and precise skill that I'd never seen before. Even my father wouldn't have managed such a result at his peak, and I stared at the cloak and hood, dismayed, when thoughts of just how much money went into this cluttered my mind.

Rowena expected me to wear this in the damp morning fog? And that was only for a brief walk from the house to the main road and then back? Surely my shabby old coat would do, I thought, balking, but I also remembered the look of grave determination on Rowena's face when she firmly insisted I wore the cloak. I had to sigh and move the cloak to the armchair, where I draped it carefully over the backrest.

You're getting paid handsomely to attend to the lady, odd whims and habits aside. Remember your father. What's another day spent indulging the harmless wishes of a lonely spinster who's clearly ill and possibly getting worse with time?

Sleep was uneventful that night, and I woke up the following morning feeling quite refreshed and even eager to work. A quick look out the window gave me a fog-choked world, but at least the rains had stopped completely.

Breakfast was a solitary affair again, but I was immediately summoned to Rowena's study, where she handed me the letter I wrote last night.

"Now then," she said. "As I mentioned yesterday, I have a man come around at eight-thirty once a week to pick up any post that never makes it into Mr. Grieve's hands. He never enters the drive and will simply stop at the entrance and take letters from whomever happens to be standing there. I usually have one of the maids do it before, but they're needed more within doors despite such a brief and easy task. I'll be depending upon you from this day forward to take care of this. Do you understand, Edgar?"

"I do. Does the man come in all weather?"

"Ah, no. He's loyal and hard-working, to be sure, my dear, but he isn't mad." Rowena offered me one of her youthful smiles. "And I've impressed upon him the importance of taking good care of himself first. If the weather's too harsh, I simply hold on to my letters have Mr. Grieve take them. None of my correspondences were ever urgent—a much-appreciated luxury for a woman in my position—and I don't see them changing anytime soon. You'll learn quickly enough that things move very idly around here—for better or for worse, one might say."

I nodded. "I should get ready."

"Indeed. The cloak I gave you will keep you warm. I daresay it will suit you perfectly, but do let me know if the fit isn't right. That's an easy thing to fix.

Carry on now." Another lazy flick of her thin wrist, and I was off and hastening down the passageway to my room.

I threw on the cloak and hood and observed myself in a cheval mirror standing beside my wardrobe. I blinked upon realizing that mirror wasn't there before, which meant it had been brought up while I was having breakfast. Or perhaps it had been moved from another room for just this reason, I thought, screwing my face wryly as my mind drifted back to my time reading to Rowena yesterday. The recamier upon which she'd theatrically draped herself had also been brought into the drawing-room for that purpose.

It was a very strange notion, indeed, that Rowena would be so particular about how a moment unfolded. It seemed as though she'd had a precise idea on how something—however casual or mundane as to be inconsequential in normal circumstances—ought to appear. The more I considered yesterday's reading, in fact, the more I was convinced it was an intricately choreographed moment that went down to the hypothetical fraction of an inch in an effort at bringing to life a specific picture Rowena's fertile imagination had woven.

And now this—a cloak and hood meant for heroes in romantic novels—purposefully chosen for me for an ordinary task with a cheval mirror brought into my room to ensure I wore it properly. How was I supposed to look in it, anyway? I pursed my lips in thought this time as I studied myself, torn between confusion and wonder because while a part of me was mortified by my overly theatrical appearance, another part of me was quite astonished at the effect.

Indeed, the longer I studied myself, the more I felt like I *should* be in a romantic novel. It was simply the way the cloak hung down around me that gave me such a wild idea.

And it took a bit of effort for me to extricate myself from such an idiotic fancy and hurry out. It would be eight-thirty soon, and with the fog so thick and sluggish, I knew I needed to take good care walking down the drive toward the main road.

The gray morning was awfully cold, and I had to pull the cloak more tightly around me as I gingerly picked my way past muddy puddles and the occasional rock protruding from the rain-soaked ground. The fog swirled as I moved through, the fresh air quite pleasing to breathe in, the gentle chirping of unseen birds offering me some comfort as my confidence grew the closer I got to the main road. The sunlit and airy wood I admired looked more like a gathering of mute specters keeping guard over the flower field, and I couldn't help but shiver a little at the sudden awareness of being keenly observed.

I reached the point where the drive joined the main road. There I stood for a time, waiting and feeling less and less anchored to reality given the fantastical nature of my surroundings—not to mention my own appearance and dress. And like a hero in a romantic novel, I waited and fretted until the slow and steady clopping of a horse's hooves broke through the thick silence.

A shadow formed in the distance, darkening and taking a more distinctive shape until horse and rider took a leisurely stroll toward me.

"Are you Mrs. Fairclough's new assistant?" the man demanded, his voice gruff as he drew up. Up close, his ordinary appearance resettled me, and I had to blink as though I'd just emerged from a mystifying dream.

"I am."

He reached out a thick, rough hand. "The letter, if you please."

I obliged readily enough, and with a curt thanks, the man stuffed the letter in a soiled old satchel hanging across his body and then went on his way. The interaction itself was brief and abrupt, and I was soon left standing alone and gaping stupidly at the fog-covered countryside, the horse's lazy progress fading in the distance.

I wasn't as lost in fancy on my way back to the house, though the fog continued its hold on the area. Bridewater House loomed ahead, a mournful shade peering out sullenly from the steadily thickening cobwebs time continued to spin around it. I gazed at the dark and lifeless windows for a time, barely aware of what I was staring at until something drew me attention to one on the upper floor.

A white face looked out, I thought, barely discernible in the dim light of the gloomy morning. As I drew closer, however, I noticed the pale eyes and the keen and almost hungry attention being directed at me.

Rowena Fairclough watched me, unmoving, from the window, and even from a distance, I could feel the hopeless yearning in her gaze. I didn't think it was anything like lust or attraction; in fact, something about that eager, needy stare told me it was quite the opposite. That there was, I felt, something about *me* at that precise moment that Rowena desperately wanted. Something I somehow represented to her by moving about in a foggy morning wearing an old-fashioned cloak and hood.

My steps faltered at the thought, and I paused in my walk back and gazed up at the window, meeting her bold and unwavering appraisal with a questioning look. I didn't know how long we regarded each other thus, but the spell was eventually broken at the sound of another horse approaching the house, this time making its way up the drive.

Rowena didn't even blink or look startled let alone self-conscious. She merely moved her gaze from me to someone behind before stepping away from the window without another look my way.

"Ah—good morning, Edgar."

I turned around to find Cyrille approaching me with an astonished smile. "Good morning," I stammered, coloring.

"What on earth are you wearing?"

"Oh. Um—Mrs. Fairclough told me to wear this. For a job, you see. Um—I posted a letter?" Lord, I must have looked so stupid then. "I look ridiculous, don't I?"

Cyrille laughed. "I met the fellow on my way here. He mentioned you though perhaps in somewhat startled tones. No need to fret—he was expecting one of the maids, I think. They might have been enjoying a bit of flirtation."

I grinned in spite of myself. What cheek this man had, I thought. "Well, I'm awfully sorry I was a disappointment, then."

Cyrille's smile softened. Then he climbed down from his horse and stood before me, the smile still there. He gently brushed away a lock of hair that had refused to be confined under the hood and dipped over my brows.

"Hardly a disappointment," he said, his voice dropping somewhat. In a slightly louder volume, he asked, "Have you had breakfast yet?"

"I have. But they're all waiting for you inside, and there's still food laid out if you're hungry."

"Excellent. Pray escort me and my poor horse to Rowena's castle. I've never thought to saunter idly down this drive in such a dreadful fog, but I've also never expected to be met by anyone half so beguiling. Let's take a full hour to cover the final few yards, Edgar."

I opened my mouth and then shut it, took a deep breath, and found my tongue loosened at last. "That's rather bold of you," I retorted though without heat.

"I'm an artist. I recognize, appreciate, and celebrate beauty in ways that shock proper society. Everyone here knows that, my dear, and no one cares as long as I—well—do the right sort of art. Indeed, I've kept myself busy while away. You shall find out how soon enough."

What on earth could anyone say to that? I certainly had no idea and was obliged to shut up.

My face could have burst into flames, taking my hair and everything else with it if this man kept up his flirtations. I'd never had this sort of interaction before—and in open space at that! I hoped no one within doors had been watching us the whole time though I knew I never once invited such brazen expressions. I remembered my schoolfellows occasionally whispering about brief and innocent romances, but I'd assumed they all outgrew any turns to experimentation in such closed off quarters.

But to have someone like Cyrille Boivin say these things to me without batting an eye and without hesitation or faltering—I'd be surprised if my brain could untangle itself from the tight knots it wound itself into. So I did what any sane person would have done under similar circumstances.

The moment Mrs. Quigg opened the front door, I excused myself and bolted right past her and went straight for the stairs and my room. That I was able to escape so quickly without tripping over the long cloak and causing myself a good deal of mischief was a miracle. And that ridiculous cloak was off me in a second though I remembered nothing of the moment I rid myself of its cumbersome weight.

Chapter 14

The next few days went by differently from the previous ones thanks to Cyrille's most welcome presence and the sunshine he'd brought with him—quite literally. Rowena, buoyed by her artist's return, immediately commandeered Cyrille's attention, and the pair spent many hours in the studio with Rowena moving back and forth dressed in a variety of costumes.

Her new series of paintings was well underway, I was told, and she was expected to keep Cyrille busy with her new schemes. As to what they spent so much time on, I learned it was all about preliminary sketches, notes, and a great deal of discussion between artist and patroness. Both, I reckoned, were quite particular and likely disagreed more than found common ground.

Cyrille, I also learned, had his own bedroom in Bridewater House, situated in Rowena's wing and in the extreme opposite of mine. It was a corner room as well, and he also kept a pretty expansive wardrobe there in the event he needed to stay for more than a couple of days because of his work. It certainly made a good deal of sense to have one's private artist hang about the premises when fully immersed in a commission—particularly one that required so much of his time as to make any journey home a right nuisance.

Now and then I observed them retreating to the privacy of the temple with Cyrille carrying a note-book with him, and there they talked at length. I was never invited at any time for those, and I truly didn't mind at all. With the sun finally breaking through and chasing the gloomy clouds away, I was at liberty to explore and enjoy the property. I wanted to spend as much time outdoors as I possibly could, given my recent experiences within.

Rowena's mood enjoyed an equal burst of optimism and giddiness that bubbled out in conversation frequently. Her features still retained their ghostly pale quality, her unnervingly light eyes still had about them an otherworldliness that made me think she could see things no one else could, and her demands for reading time grew more frequent. When before I was ordered to read to her in the early to mid-afternoon, Cyrille's return seemed to have unleashed a hunger in her for what I now referred to as "staged reading", and I was soon reading into the late hours with only the candelabra and modest fire helping my efforts.

"Sit over there by the lamp in the corner, Edgar."

"Lie on your stomach, my dear, just where the sunlight touches the floor. Don't fret—there's a new rug I specifically ordered to be cleaned and moved here for this purpose."

"Splendid! You look exquisite with the candle light on you just so."

"Do tousle your hair a bit, my dear. A pretty, windswept look becomes you."

It took a bit of time, but I eventually grew comfortable enough doing my job in spite of the eccentricities that defined it. Perhaps it was nothing more than Cyrille's influence because having one more person there truly helped me as well, and I didn't feel quite alone anymore even when he was somewhere else in the house.

The happier effects of his presence on Rowena cascaded among the servants, and I heard distant voices every now and then when before it was nothing but a soul-crippling silence bearing down on me. It was remarkable.

The sun's return came with warming temperatures as spring waned and prepared the land for summer's entrance. I thought then to bring a book out and choose one of the benches so cleverly placed along the stone walk encircling such a massive house.

A pair of urns flanked each bench, and out of those urns a lush and fully contained flowering shrub burst. It was yet another one of Rowena's picturesque touches—deliberate and carefully planned, I daresay—which lent the immediate area surrounding the great house a beautifully designed accent. There were so many of those charming groupings of benches and urns along the walk that it took me a while to choose one.

And for the next several minutes I sat there, quite engrossed in the book, all but losing track of time as written adventures lured me away from the reality of my present world. Every now and then I'd glance up and sigh in contentment, taking in deep, rejuvenating breaths and enjoying the sight of a stately, ivy-covered house on one side and a sprawling field of flowers on the other. The sparse wood bordering the entire property beckoned to me as well, but I chose to ignore their enticing call for the time being.

I tried to avoid being alone with Cyrille despite his cheerful and most welcome company. The preposterous expression of attraction in the morning fog a week ago lingered in my mind, and whenever the memory came to me unbidden, I found I couldn't meet anyone's eye while my face warmed. And yet I also grew to realize that I tended to seek him out and observe him in some confusion from a distance.

I'd glance at him surreptitiously every now and then at the dinner-table while he and Rowena were lost in their usual friendly chatter. I'd peer out of the upper-floor rear windows on my way out of the library in hopes of catching him in the midst of a leisurely stroll to or from the temple, Rowena hanging on to his every word. I'd wait with bated breath to hear his laughter or his voice raised in a happy and energetic exchange from somewhere in the house.

And it certainly didn't help that he showed me exactly what it was that had kept him busy while he was away. It had been thoughts of me, judging from the sudden explosion of sketches of me in various poses and candid moments. Most of them were slipped between pages of books I carried with me, and even one had found its way into my room—lying upon my pillow.

It was awful and exhilarating beyond reason, and I didn't have anyone to talk to about this. I never dared to broach the subject of other schoolboys' attempts at courting me in school with my father, and now it seemed as though my past had come back, more dreadful and pressing than ever. Over a week after Cyrille's return to Bridewater House, I was well convinced of my own infatuation with him.

And perhaps the most dreadful thing about this mess was the fact that I'd cluttered my mind so much with thoughts of him that I had a most difficult time keeping my head on my task.

"Whatever on earth is wrong with you today?" Rowena demanded while I lost my place in the book I was reading to her one morning. Cyrille was nowhere near, by the bye, having withdrawn straight to the studio following breakfast.

"I'm sorry. I'm just having a terrible time concentrating today," I stammered weakly. "May I start over?"

Rowena scoffed, eyes blazing, and she straightened up in her recamier with an air so offended, I was terrified of being dismissed entirely and sent packing that very moment. I had to scramble from my place on the floor with apologies spilling out of me.

"What's all this? Are you ill and haven't told me?"

I shook my head, unable to meet Rowena's angry gaze. "No, ma'am."

"Are you overwhelmed? Bored? Restless?" When I mutely shook my head, she jerked hers toward the windows. "Go on then. I suppose you've earned a proper day of rest and time for yourself. It's a sunny day out, it's fairly warm, and you can bring a book with you."

"Yes, ma'am."

Her mouth flattened at my nervous reversal to "ma'am", but at least she didn't pursue the matter. All the same, as I was about to leave the drawing-room, she called out another set of instructions.

"Sit on the bench closest to the wood on the north end of the house."

I stared at her for a few seconds, waiting for more, but she just raised a brow at me in the most imperious way and then turned away. I sighed and left, taking the book with me.

There were two benches on the north end of the house, and I decided to sit on the one I felt stood closest to the wood. It took me a moment to compose myself following a mental flagellation for being such an utter blockhead in front of my employer.

How could I let another person distract me to such an extent? Rowena was strict in her requirements though she did temper her demands and behavior whenever she saw fit, but I was specifically chosen for a job that kept my father alive and a roof over his head. Allowing daydreams to carry me off to some stupidly fantastical worlds was unforgivable no matter how eccentric Rowena's commands were.

I blinked away the threat of angry tears, shook myself back to reason, and promptly lost myself in my book. It wasn't the same book of poetry I'd been entertaining Rowena with. She'd already moved on to something else—a romantic novel this time—after nearly a week of verses, and I never got to finish Wordsworth's poem. It had grown too tedious for her to listen to though I quite enjoyed the rustic images the poet's skillful pen had woven in my head. A day after Cyrille's arrival, I was ordered back to the library for something "far more entertaining than a dead man's ode to a dead world".

I'd decided Ann Radcliffe would be a much better fit for her, and she seemed to agree.

I lost myself in Mrs. Radcliffe's wild imagination and all the horrible trappings of her novel until the heat of the sun as it crept across the sky grew intolerable, and I was obliged to stop and mark my progress.

A glance at the nearby wood convinced me to stretch my legs and explore the trees, so I gladly went forward. The widely spaced trees created an environment that turned out to be just as magical as I'd expected, with the sunlight streaming through branches and carpeting the ground with a pleasant glow. Birdsong was all around me, and I took an idle stroll through the trees, following the wood's progress around the flower field's perimeter and toward the back, where the temple stood.

All was calm and soothing, a much-needed source of comfort following my earlier humiliation and shameful retreat. Cyrille never entered my thoughts throughout my walk—a good thing, really, because I couldn't be distracted by the magical quality of the wood, the pretty flower field it protected, and the ivy-cloaked house standing not too far away.

I went back inside when fatigue took over, and the need for a thorough wash and a change of clothes beckoned. I'd been told that I could always request for a pail of water and not just a ewer for a full soapy scrub and so fumbled my way to the kitchen to ask for one from Mrs. Quigg.

"Oh—no need, my dear," she said with a pleased grin. "There's already one waiting for you in your room."

"There is?"

"Indeed there is. My mistress specifically requested one when you went out for your walk. She's quite good at anticipating everyone's needs, you know. Will you be requiring more towels, do you think? One of the girls brought a fresh set for you."

"No, thank you. That's very kind, Mrs. Quigg."

"Oh, bless you, child. Don't thank me. It's Mrs. Fairclough's wish, and you know she always gets it, especially when it involves you."

I blinked. "Me? I don't understand."

"Why, the lady's dreadfully fond of you, my dear. Haven't you even noticed that? My word—you're such an innocent. But I suppose this can also come from growing up without a mother. See, the lack of a lady's affection can skew a boy's perceptions on how the fair sex is expected to relate to him. Tut, tut! What a shame, indeed. Now go on, my dear. Clean up and rest if you need a bit of a nap. Lunch will be ready in an hour."

I found the pail of water and a fresh pile of towels waiting for me in my room. My ewer was also filled, the wash basin cleaned and dried. I quickly stripped down to nothing and washed myself as thoroughly as I could, feeling the lingering effects of my earlier distress scatter with every rub of the wet, soapy towel.

A pleasing lethargy took its place, and once I dried myself, I went to the wardrobe and sorted out what to wear. A nap sounded very good to me at the moment, but I did assemble a proper suit for lunch and the rest of the day.

Once dressed in a clean shirt and trousers, threw open my windows to allow some fresh air through, delighting in the breeze that blew in and lifted my spirits. The sleepiness that had taken hold deepened, and I was soon yawning loudly and fumbling for my bed.

Then I froze.

My bedroom door stood wide open though I knew I shut it completely behind me. I never heard it creak open on its old hinges, which was a sound I'd grown quite used to. It was certainly opened just now because I'd glimpsed the door while dressing, and I recall it being closed still. I regarded the door in stunned silence for a moment before the knowledge set in—a familiar and awful realization dawning, an experience I'd had not too long ago back in the library.

It was the awareness of someone being in the room with me. I instantly held my breath, waiting and listening, wondering if soft, stealthy footsteps on old floorboards would soon make themselves heard. At length something did catch my attention, and it wasn't a quietly groaning board. It was a light, almost inarticulate sound—the sort of sound I'd gotten used to as a little boy at play. The sound of a toy ball rolling across the floor.

A terrible eternity seemed to pass before the sound stopped, and after another moment waiting, I mustered the courage to creep forward and around the bed, my eyes glued to the open door, until I stood close enough to see just beyond it. A child's old ball sat before my bedroom door, slightly rocking as a ball would when it encountered resistance.

Chapter 15

There was no one in the hallway, of course. My heart thundered, and my skin crawled. I'd stopped thinking about these inexplicable moments when Cyrille arrived, and it seemed the house read my heart and decided to sink back into silence and slumber for a bit. Now whatever it was that had been trying to get my attention had grown weary of waiting for me to get over my unwanted infatuation with our resident artist.

I picked up the ball and weighed it. It was quite ordinary, much to my surprise, though most certainly old. It seemed to have enjoyed a good deal of proper use judging from the scratches and weathered spots on its surface. I took a deep breath, hoping to regain my composure, but my effort failed. I stood just outside my bedroom with my hair standing on end and my blood roaring in my ears.

I knew with a terrible certainty that I was being shadowed by a ghost.

"Who are you?" I asked in a trembling voice. "What do you need from me?"

Nothing but silence answered. Muted light coming from empty rooms with their own doors thrown open eased the dimness of the hallway. Stone nymphs kept their silent vigil and lent the eerie stillness an air of watchfulness that left me growing more and more anxious.

There was a guardedness in the silence. I couldn't help but feel a pair of invisible eyes fixed upon me with keen interest. Friendly interest? I didn't know—wouldn't have been able to tell either way. My hold on the ball tightened, my hand cold and trembling.

"I have your toy. What would you like me to do with it?" Another moment of dreadful silence followed. "Where are you?"

Here!

I nearly dropped the ball then. I took in a ragged breath and then two, suddenly noticing the faint cloud puffs coming out of my mouth. The air around me had gone cold though I was sure it was nowhere near the chill that now infused my blood. But when I spoke again, I was shocked at how calm my voice sounded. How controlled, even. How on earth I managed it, I didn't know, but I somehow did.

"Who are you?" I asked.

I glanced around, my gaze moving past the silent passageway and its mute guardians and into my bedroom where sunlight poured in.

Where is my mamma?

"I don't know where she is, I'm afraid. Where are you?"

Here!

The voice—it was most certainly a little child's voice. A boy, I think, but it wove in and out of hearing, and even then, I could barely catch it when it did fight to be heard. I couldn't tell how close the child—the ghost—was. The voice alone sounded so far away and yet not, dispersed yet focused, leaving me utterly confused as to its source.

The cloud puffs were slowly weakening, and worry seized me at the thought of losing such a tenuous connection. That poor, tiny voice—so soft, so lonely—touched me in a way that surprised me and compelled me to try harder.

I knelt on the floor and held out the ball. "Is this yours? I can't play with you if I can't see you, you know. What's your name?"

I uncurled my fingers and waited. The ball lightly shivered and then was gently pushed off my hand, landing on the floor with a dull thump and then rolling a couple of feet away. The chill in the air vanished, and whatever terrible silence had been there before was now replaced by light chirping outside my bedroom windows. The child had gone.

It took me a moment to gather my wits and bring my heartbeats down to a steadier rhythm, and I stumbled to my feet and gathered the ball. Lost in thought, I went back in my bedroom and set the ball on my writing-desk before stretching out on my bed. Terror had turned to worry as I replayed the incident over and over in my head while chasing after ideas about the child and his identity.

I'd never experienced a haunting before. All knowledge of ghosts and supernatural things were from fireside tales and the occasional story meant to keep me well-behaved by an exhausted father. This child had reached out to me, and I was now certain it was he who'd shadowed my steps in the library, held my hand in the dark. And now that I'd experienced another unseen encounter with him in the light of day, whatever terror that had been unleashed before was now gone, replaced by pity and sadness.

The sudden appearance of the toy soldier, the ball, the creeping footsteps, and the shy handhold—none of those indicated a soul intent upon driving the living away. There was a timidity and an uncertainty to those moments, the barely audible whispers hinting at a child who was seeking a loved one long gone.

It must be companionship the poor creature desired though he could be far better off moving toward whatever world awaited us on our deaths. Moving among the living, he wouldn't be seen, and had I been of a much more nervous sort, he'd have suffered even greater rejection and shunning. There would be no peace for him here.

I blinked and then frowned as I stared up at the intricately carved canopy above me.

"Mrs. Quigg knows," I murmured. I'd just remembered that brief glimpse of her throwing the toy soldier into the fire and behaving as though nothing happened afterward. Would she have lied to me later had I pursued the issue? Would she reassure me with false claims of returning the toy to one of the maids?

I found then that I couldn't rest and so sprang out of bed, hastily dressed, and went downstairs in search of the housekeeper. I found her wandering the hallway downstairs, entering every room and ensuring each was cleaned and tidied to her satisfaction.

"Mrs. Quigg, I know it sounds ridiculous, but—but I'm being haunted by a little boy."

She glanced over her shoulder at me, a placid look on her face, before turning her attention back to giving the gold frame she was dusting a gentle wipe with her rag.

"Hmm. Ignore him, dear. Don't let him chase you off the way he did the others." At my startled little sound, she shrugged and moved on to the next framed portrait. She gazed at it in fond silence for a second or two before gently wiping the bottom edge, which gathered dust the most. "Yes, there were others before you. All young ladies, of course, but they proved to be too nervous and too prone to hysterics."

I wasn't sure what to make of the conversation because Mrs. Quigg spoke with hardly a spark of emotion. She merely laid out the facts and left it at that—quite dispassionate and puzzling in how unfeeling she could be about it.

"Is that why Mrs. Fairclough looked for a male assistant this time?"

"Perhaps. It's very likely if you think about it. I simply do as my mistress bids me." Another dispassionate shrug followed.

"But who is he?" I prodded. "He's been giving me toys..."

"Has he now? Well, I suppose children will seek someone to play with. As I said, young man, ignore him."

"He was looking for his mother."

Mrs. Quigg's movements paused briefly but carried on as though nothing just surprised her to silence. "Of course he would. He died young, obviously."

"But..."

She turned around then and leveled me with a patient and indulgent stare. No smile touched features, and there was a motherly firmness and mild disapproval there that compelled me to shut up.

"Mr. Cushing, just carry on with your work. Your purpose here is to do what Mrs. Fairclough tells you, and that's that. The ghost is around, it will make its presence known, and it will try to reach out to you for whatever irrational reason only the restless dead might have. If it continues to bother you with gifts, throw every one of them in the fire." She seemed to read my mind as I frowned at her. "I threw that doll in the fire and was forced to lie to you before because I didn't want to alarm you. Now that you know the truth, I expect you to do as you're told or let us know now that a haunted house frightens you, and we won't waste any more time keeping you here."

"I'm not frightened of the child," I blurted out, affronted.

"Excellent. Mrs. Fairclough's in a most fragile state of health, as you already know, and the last thing I want to do is to urge you to leave and start over with our search for a proper assistant. The lady's been through too much as it is, and she isn't getting any younger."

"Yes, ma'am."

Mrs. Quigg smiled then, her figure easing, and then swept her gaze around her. "Isn't this room just a marvel? Mrs. Fairclough has such exquisite taste, and it's always a pleasure looking after her possessions. If each piece that others call inconsequential makes her happy, it falls on us to make sure every one of them is properly cared for and allowed its place of honor in such a house."

"Yes, ma'am."

"I expect nothing less."

I nodded, still frowning. Then I withdrew, the conversation refusing to ease its hold on my mind. I truly didn't know what to make of it—of Mrs. Quigg's clear indifference to a dead child. I didn't know what the ghost's connection to Rowena and the house was, and Mrs. Quigg played the keeper of her mistress's secrets.

I simply didn't know where else to go for my questions—if any mystery existed at all. I suppose it would be a mystery to me and only me since the housekeeper and the mistress were both players in some odd drama.

"Cyrille, then?" I muttered as I stood on the ground floor landing, gazing up at the grand staircase. "Surely he'd know something."

After all, he was the third of his family to be hired by Rowena. Perhaps something had been said among them regarding Bridewater House's peculiarities and especially its owner's history. I regarded the ostentatiousness of my environment in thoughtful silence. The choice in furnishings, bits and bobs, statuary, and paintings. Even the property outside wasn't spared a deliberate design.

Everything about the house screamed "fantasy" to me. The structure's architecture, the things it contained, the fact that it had been built around an artist's studio. Rowena had the money, and she had no family to hold her back. No husband, especially. And now that she was older and clearly fading in health, this singular world of hers meant a great deal more than ever, served a clearer purpose over time.

The studio was the heart of Bridewater House, Mrs. Quigg had once said. I suspected it was because of all the art that came out of it. Every painting was a defiant strike against mortality. For every day her health faded, Rowena had a dreamscape in oil keeping her youth and vibrancy alive, and she would die and live forever.

And how did the ghost come into the picture? A member of the family, then?

The rest of the day went rather quickly. Lunch was served, but I was alone because artist and patroness were still in the studio, and neither emerged till after tea. Mrs. Quigg reassured me that they were brought a tray of food, and they often ate in the studio.

Then I was again summoned for tea and a book, Cyrille nowhere in sight. He'd been told to go to his room and rest given the intense work he was subjected to all day. He wasn't expected down for dinner, either, and Rowena forbade me from interacting with him for the rest of the day.

I suppose I'd have to wait till tomorrow to ask him about Rowena's past.

My time with Rowena that afternoon was exhausting on the whole. She was again distracted in her head, her attention barely on me even with her ordering me to arrange myself upon the window seat, even tousling my hair again and taking off my jacket, cravat, and shoes and looking for all the world like an indolent schoolboy idly reading against the fading afternoon light.

Now and then I'd steal glances at Rowena, who'd seated herself on the loveseat, her skirts properly spread out and her posture relaxed, but there was a subtle tension in her air. It was as though she were waiting for some unknown signal that would summon her and make her spring to her feet and run off. Her eyes were fixed upon me, but I knew her mind was elsewhere. All the same, I carried on until she told me to stop and complained of not feeling well and needing to retire until dinner.

With the night skies as clear as they were in the day, I thought to take a moonlit walk along the drive. The chirping crickets and the gentle night breeze soothed me, chased away any superstitious terrors that might grip me. Before long I'd reached the end of the drive and turned back with my mind and heart full of my poor father. I couldn't remember what it was exactly I thought about, but it diverted me long enough to reach a point on the drive where I could look up and catch sight of anything framed by the upper floor windows.

A flickering light moved slowly around one room and then another. I knew it was Mrs. Quigg making her nightly inspection of the rooms she so adored. Like a soldier guarding the ramparts, I couldn't help but note. Fierce in her loyalty, perhaps ruthless in her methods of protecting her beloved mistress.

Chapter 16

I awoke the following morning with lingering impressions—not dreams, I argued with myself—of having someone in bed with me. I'd already expected something quite terrifying while preparing for sleep. After shedding my clothes, giving my face a final quick wash, and throwing my nightshirt on, I'd turned around to find the bedroom door once again standing ajar though it had been securely shut and *locked* just a moment ago.

I knew then that I was in for a midnight visit from my new friend. I shut and locked the door again, ignoring the awful darkness of the upper-floor hallway, and then blew my candle out and crawled into bed. Nothing happened for a time, and I soon drifted off. As wakefulness fled, though, I was distantly aware of a palpable change in the room's temperature. It slowly dropped until I was obliged to slide further under my blankets, barely noticing the faint cloudy puffs escaping my mouth.

I'd locked myself in my room with a dead child, I thought, and it was the last thing I told myself before sleep claimed me. The last thing I knew that wasn't part of a dream as well was of slight movement on the bedclothes as though something quite light had just climbed up onto it. There was the subtle dipping of the mattress and then the unnerving feeling—no, knowledge, more likely—of someone curling up on the bed close to me.

There was no invisible hand reaching out and feeling for mine. For that, I was grateful despite my acceptance of the reality of a child's ghost haunting Bridewater House. Haunting *me*. But the presence certainly made itself felt even as a wild mix of sensations that chased after my fading consciousness.

I went to sleep then only faintly terrified because one couldn't ignore being in bed with the specter of a long-dead person. Whether or not the knowledge of not being alone affected my dreams afterward, I couldn't say. I remembered nothing of them if I did dream.

And when the sun rose, whatever remaining influence crumbled to nothing, and I emerged from my bedroom feeling a bit melancholy. Again, as before, I was struck by the lack of a threat from the ghost. Even though I fell asleep not fully at ease given the eeriness of the moment, I was still affected by the loneliness that seemed to define the ghost's presence and, especially, movements.

In the clear light of day, I managed to consider the poor creature's restlessness and his constant yearning for companionship. The shyly held hand, the meek and furtive footsteps along the passageway, the offering of toys, and now the climbing onto the bed...

I could easily imagine myself doing just that when I was a little boy. I could even remember a handful of moments during which I'd done such things because I needed to be with my father. At least in my case, I'd been fortunate enough to be blessed with a father who loved me.

The ghost, however? I couldn't say with any certainty because I could get nothing from Mrs. Quigg about the unfortunate boy's history and his connection to Bridewater House. But the yearning was there—the innocent hope of being welcomed or needed by someone else, very typical of children, I daresay.

I now wondered if the boy had been neglected when alive. If he managed to ask for his mother in answer to my question, I reckoned his restlessness in death was caused by his missing parent.

And so my mind was very much occupied throughout breakfast, which was once again a solitary event. This time, however, I didn't feel up to the task of being in anyone's company—even Cyrille's, for that matter, though the man's impishly smiling visage certainly occupied my thoughts a good deal all of yesterday. I was informed that he and Rowena were once more back in the studio, lost to the world until they decided to end that day's session.

"Oh, I honestly don't know what the gentleman's been up to," Mrs. Quigg blurted out in a rush of words edged with frustration on her mistress's behalf. "As far as I've seen, no real progress has been done on anything—even that painting my poor lady's sat for in the past. Her shepherdess painting, I mean."

"Maybe he's having a difficult time with it?"

"Quite likely. He's never been stuck like this before, you know. But whatever his excuse, he'd best get over it and give my lady the results he's promised. All he's been giving her are these miniatures and small watercolor pieces—really, what can one do with those things?"

I went upstairs to the library, intent upon exploring other volumes for my own reading pleasure now that I had Radcliffe's novel already in progress for Rowena. I hesitated at the door, my skin prickling a little when the memory of that moment not too long ago with the ghost's unseen hand clasping mine in the gloom arose. I knew better now, though, and I managed to shake off the unease and move swiftly inside.

And before long I was perched on the top rung of one of the rolling ladders, perusing a book and weighing its worth.

"She watches you, you know."

I looked up with a start and found Cyrille leaning against the doorframe and watching me intently. He'd taken off his artist's apron and appeared without his jacket, his sleeves rolled up to his elbows, his cravat and waistcoat missing, his shirt undone at the collar. His hair was messy, and while I couldn't see finer details from where I sat, I suspected he also sported several tiny spots of paint on his hair and face.

"What?" I stammered.

"Rowena. She watches you. Especially when she sends you out for a walk or for a quiet read. It's no different from when you read to her, and she tells you to sit or lie somewhere specific."

Cyrille shrugged and then pushed himself away from the doorframe to saunter inside, his gaze fixed upon me as he moved closer. Then he paused at the bottom of the rolling ladder and waited there, his hands grasping the hand rails while he observed me keenly from below, clearly waiting for my response to such a startling claim.

"But—why on earth would she do that? This isn't like a theater or anything. I'm not performing in a play."

"You might as well be, I suppose, but that's neither here nor there."

"What about the ones who came before me? Did she do the same with them?"

Cyrille's intent look melted into one of surprise. "Ah—so you know about the others. I've a feeling Mrs. Quigg told you, which also makes me wonder if something's happened that forced that bit of truth out of her."

"I pressed her about—about something." I blushed, suddenly wondering if I should drop a hint about my unearthly companion. "And that came out in conversation."

Cyrille nodded. "There were others before you, yes. Three or four young ladies, I think, but I can't remember how many exactly. None lasted more than a month."

"Do you know why?" I asked, watching him closely.

"They all felt uneasy living here. I don't blame them, really. You know how the house is inside, and I'm sure you've already wondered about the artificiality of the outside as well."

Cyrille then slowly ascended the ladder, making it shudder under our combined weight, and I tightened my grip on the rail while pressing the book I'd pulled out tightly against my chest. As though doing that would help me in a disastrous collapse of a rolling ladder!

"Stop," I cried. "I don't think this ladder can hold us both!"

He didn't, of course, and a mischievous smile bloomed on his face, making him even more roguish than ever. Once he was close enough, he gently pushed my knees apart and moved into the awfully limited space between my legs until our faces were properly aligned. Under me, the ladder groaned and creaked but held firm.

"I'm sure you've wondered by now if our dear Mrs. Fairclough was mad," he murmured. The smile lingered, and he was so, so close to me that I could barely breathe from his proximity. "She is—to a point, I daresay. I'm sure there's no need for me to elaborate on the sort of obsessive mania she harbors toward the fantastical and the immortal."

I could only swallow and nod, my eyes wide and unblinking.

"If I were you, I'd pack my clothes and run as far away as I could before she does something we'll all regret."

He paused for a second or two, appearing to consider something, and then settled on a decision. He leaned forward and pressed a kiss against my lips—a soft and gentle peck once and then twice, testing the waters, I think, before surging into a demanding pressure that forced my lips apart and allowed his tongue unexpected entry into my mouth.

I blinked stupidly for a second before yielding to him entirely, the foreign feeling of someone else's mouth and tongue moving against my own clouding my brain and rendering me quite dumb from shock and, yes, pleasure. My heart fluttered as madly as my stomach.

The kiss was over too soon though Cyrille's handsome features still hovered very close to mine. When he spoke again, his voice came out in breathless whispers.

"I don't want to see you get dragged into her make-believe world, Edgar," he said. "I don't want to see you trapped forever in one of her absurdist paintings.

She surrounds herself with beauty, and when she sees something she likes, she'll move heaven and hell to make it hers. You, my dear, are exactly that—beautiful."

He traced my mouth with his fingers.

"Perfection, even. She's already begun to watch you closely. She's made you position yourself in specific ways just to read her a goddamned book. She's already begun to pretend you're a part of her world—her world as in the one she's slowly, slowly sinking into because she can't help it, and she loves it too well to remove herself from it completely."

I shook my head in disbelief. This was all to outlandish to be true though Cyrille's earnest and even eager manner told me he believed in what he was telling me.

"Don't believe me, do you? Tell me, my sweet innocent, what letters has she asked you to write?"

"Why?"

"Just answer my question, please."

He nipped my lower lip and drew a reflexive shudder from me. So I told him, and he chuckled, this time kissing his way from my mouth to my ear. Another shudder wracked me when he whispered directly into it.

"Those gentlemen she made you write to are long dead, Edgar. They were my grandfather's professional acquaintances, and it was through him that Mrs. Fairclough knew about them and what they can offer her magnificent house as commissions."

He drew away then and placed a merciful distance between us though it also meant he could see my deeply flushed complexion and look of confusion and excitement. I couldn't even manage to breathe a single syllable if my life depended upon it.

"Just ask Mrs. Quigg if you doubt me."

"She won't say anything, I'm sure," I stammered, still red-faced and breathing irregularly. "Just like she didn't want to tell me more about the boy."

Cyrille looked confused at first before realization caught up. Then he sighed and nodded. "Of course. *Him.* The child wandering the hallways unseen."

At the little sound of surprise I made, Cyrille shook his head again.

"I know about him—the ghost? Yes, I do. I've felt him sometimes but always so faintly—as though he hesitates to make his presence fully known and hides himself in the shadows, content to watch. And..." He appeared to catch himself then. "Well, I know about him, yes."

I nearly told him everything about my experiences, but something held me back. An overabundance of caution, perhaps? I regarded Cyrille in thoughtful silence and decided it wasn't the right time for me to say anything else. That I needed to exercise care because for all I knew, I was alone in this strange adventure. That Rowena, Mrs. Quigg, and Cyrille all may be playing defensively against me, who was a virtual stranger only recently allowed into the house.

Of course, there might not even be a real mystery to be solved since the ghost had never behaved like a threat. Perhaps the ghost simply *was*. Just like in many of those fireside tales Papa had told me over the years.

But what a tragic destiny it was for someone already dead—for him, a child in particular—to have rest evade him for any reason. To linger and seek something or someone out forever? It was too awful a thing to consider, and yet there I was, being shadowed by the restless dead.

Cyrille kissed me again, drawing me out of my thoughts. "Think about what I said, my dear. Anyway, I'm here because I've always wanted to kiss you as I'm sure you already know, and I was also instructed to spend time with you so I could sketch you in a variety of different activities and locations."

"I—I beg your pardon? Why?"

His face darkened, the mischievous little smile gone.

"I didn't warn you for nothing. Mrs. Fairclough wishes to see you painted next to her in some of the larger works of art already hanging."

When I failed to respond, my mouth hanging open, Cyrille stroked my cheek with so much tenderness and regret.

"She's about to carry you off into her world, Edgar, like the dark fairy she is. If you're not careful, you'll be just as much a part of Bridewater House as any piece of furniture it holds close, and I quite doubt you'll be able to extricate yourself from this terrible dreamscape she's determined to die in."

"And—and you? What about you?"

"I'm here to pay a debt owed someone, I'm afraid. But my time will come—your presence here has hastened it, in fact."

Chapter 17

Rowena confirmed Cyrille's astonishing claim of commissioning images of me worked into her recent canvases. When I first posed the question, she merely shrugged with barely a look in my direction because her attention was again divided as her pale gaze followed something that seemed to move along the walls of her study. There was nothing there, of course—not even shadows.

I sat at her desk, pen at the ready, heart thundering as Cyrille's voice whispered in my head. I was again being ordered to write another letter to someone in America this time and was set to post it the following morning.

"I see nothing wrong in including you, Edgar," Rowena said after a moment's pause. She stood up and slowly walked toward a window and peered out. "I happen to think of you as a son given all the patience and forbearance you've displayed since you entered my home. I know I'm not the easiest woman to work for, but you've managed all the same. I can only imagine how things are between you and your dear father. While I know of the troubles he's had, I also can see just how fortunate he is in having a son like you."

She spared me a hazy look before turning her attention back to the window. She even leaned a little closer to the glass as though eagerly keeping sight of something in the grounds below.

"I try my best," I replied.

"It seems to be effortless—at least from what I can see, anyway. And that can only mean it's simply in your nature to be kind and gentle to those who are—at a certain disadvantage, I suppose."

Rowena sighed and then gave a little start, her attention moving from the window to something just off to her right. I watched her track something with her eyes like before as she stood silhouetted by the cheerful light outside.

Then she inched away from the window and slowly, slowly walked along the periphery of the study, her eyes fixed on something only she could see. Mesmerized, almost, judging from the way she appeared so entranced by whatever it was, and whatever it was seemed to be crawling across the wall just ahead of her.

"I think I should call Mrs. Quigg and have her bring you something to drink," I offered when she vanished from view, passing behind my chair in a whisper of fabric and soft footfalls. Her perfume barely tickled my nose—something floral and cloying—and was gone in an instant. "Begging your pardon, but I don't think you're feeling all too well right now."

"Oh, I haven't felt well in years, my dear," she murmured from somewhere nearby. I dared not glance back, but I could hear her ghostly progress around the room. "I've tried doctors. I've traveled to clear my head. Perhaps it's a curse if you believe in such things. All I want is some peace and beauty, but it seems to be far too much for a woman to ask, isn't it? Even one with all the money most can only dream of."

"But—I think you still need some rest. Really, I can go to Mrs. Quigg for you."

"I know you can, dear. I know you can."

She sighed heavily then, stopped her progress, and I sneaked a look in her direction to find her standing near a corner of the room, facing the wall, her face tipped up. As I watched in surprise, her face continued to turn upward, and she even reached out a hand to something on the wall as though attempting to touch it. Her white fingers hovered in the air, pausing, and then she dropped her hand to her side and shook her head.

The spell, whatever it was, had broken.

"Anyway, as I was saying, I'd like M. Boivin to spend time with you. He'll be working on sketches, quick studies, and so on—whatever an artist does, anyway, to get his imagination going. Heaven knows, I've waited long enough for him to finish my shepherdess. Really, how difficult could it be for someone with his talent and pedigree?"

She paused then, and a sly smile lit up her haggard features. Between the moment I entered her study to now, she seemed to have aged twenty years.

"Yes, yes, I suppose he needs to have his imagination prodded a bit. Without resorting to base seductions that artists are notorious for, anyway. Our M. Boivin isn't immune to anyone's charms or the fiery impulse of an artistic temperament, don't you agree?"

She nodded at the blank sheets of paper in front of me. She didn't seem to notice my reddening complexion, or if she did, she didn't pay it any heed.

"Let's get going with the letter, Edgar. I've wasted enough time on idle chatter already."

And so we proceeded with the dictation—this time a professionally and courteously worded business request for fabric unique to the Americas, which Rowena likely wished to use for new costumes. I didn't know if fabric varied from continent to continent, but it seemed to be so judging from the way she laid out precise descriptions of patterns, weaves, and even dyes. I couldn't help but suspect that clothes in America weren't really all that different from clothes in England or anywhere else in Europe, but what did I really know?

Cyrille had told me Rowena's costumes and all manner of whimsical props were stored in an adjoining bedroom to hers. I wondered if the room was filled with clothes she only wore no more than five times (I reckoned), depending on how laborious the painting turned out to be.

I was curious, yes, but not so curious as to want to see for myself. There was something decidedly off-putting about housing such frivolities when they could have been taken to some kind of charity place, re-sewn, and then sold to women who'd enjoy much better and practical use from them.

We were done at length, and I was dismissed and ordered to go back to the flower field with an empty basket.

"Yellow and pink flowers this time, Edgar. I'd love to have the dining-room bursting with yellow and pink flowers starting this evening. And if you wish, go to the back as well though I doubt if you'll find as many specimens worth collecting as the front," Rowena said. Again she waved a dainty hand in dismissal. "And get Mrs. Quigg for me, dear. I'll have a draught in my room. My headache's come back, and I'm afraid I'll be needing a dose of the dear woman's magic elixir."

I went to Mrs. Quigg first to relay Rowena's request and then returned to my room to rest a bit and hope a moment's respite would work wonders on my poor head. If Rowena was now burdened with a headache, I wouldn't be too far behind at this rate.

The conversation we had in her study as well as the one I had with Cyrille in the library hammered at my brain over and over, and I saw so many loose and frayed threads begging to be taken up and somehow re-woven into a more cohesive story. I knew all I was getting were bits and pieces of Rowena's history.

As for the ghost, I was sure the poor thing fit in there somewhere, but the way Mrs. Quigg and Cyrille behaved so differently from each other to the boy's restlessness after death bothered me more than I cared to admit. Well—Mrs.

Quigg seemed a touch offended by the mention of a ghost, and Cyrille was dismissive only because he wasn't so sure about its reality, in a way. One was defensiveness, and the other one was carelessness born of doubt. At least I'd read their responses as such, anyway.

Perhaps Cyrille was also putting up a front for me—a careless enough façade to placate any nervousness I might have been feeling then. But it was always so difficult to tell with him, and it didn't help that I was falling madly in love with the gentleman following those tender kisses in the library and the little courtship watercolors he continued to slip inside books or place somewhere clever in my bedroom.

I was in the flower field sometime in the late afternoon when Cyrille deigned to join me, proudly brandishing a sketchbook and a pencil. He strode down the drive, turned into the field, and then all but ploughed his way to my side. I was busily gathering as many pink flowers as I could find then, and a magnificent cluster bloomed near the distant corner of the field, just a few feet shy of the bordering wood.

"I've come to draw you, monsieur," he announced, a brilliant grin creasing his face. "Don't mind me. I'll be unobtrusive, I swear."

I scowled at him. I was fully seated cross-legged on the ground, the flowers standing somewhere between my waist and chest. At least I wasn't wearing that ridiculous cloak again, but I was instructed not to wear my jacket because of the warmth of the afternoon sun. I felt a little exposed but at the same time grateful for the freedom from unwanted layers.

Cyrille made himself comfortable a few feet away, sitting down and winking at me when he opened his sketchbook to the page he needed to use.

"I can't behave naturally if I know you're just right there, drawing me."

"Keep your head down and avoid looking my direction, Edgar. That's all you need to do."

"But I know you're there," I protested, coloring furiously now. "You're—you're looming. You're not even trying to hide or make yourself inconspicuous." I waved my hand impatiently at him. "You're just—just *there*."

"How do you feel about doing this, Edgar? Picking flowers, I mean?"

I blinked at him. "Beg your pardon?"

When he raised his brows at me and simply waited, I had to sigh and scratch my head.

"I—don't know. I feel a little silly, to be honest. I know I'm following strange orders from her, but I also know she's not well, and I suppose if something so small as gathering specific flowers while looking a specific way pleases her, I shouldn't complain. It's all nothing more than trifling stuff if you think about it."

And she paid me well at that, I thought. Was I being hurt by following odd commands to do this or that, look this way or that, and so on? As far as I knew, no, I wasn't. Doubt had been planted in my head, though, by Cyrille in that talk we had, but my earlier time with Rowena not only confirmed what I'd already known before but also made me feel even more compassionate toward her.

She might suffer from some form of mania, but she was also alone save for the loyal Mrs. Quigg. She was a spinster with more money than she knew what to do with other than burn every bit of it on frivolous artwork capturing scenes from fairy tales and myths that made her happy.

I witnessed first-hand that she was also seeing things or fancying seeing things. I began to suspect the little boy's ghost was deeply tied to her, but whether or not he'd been some sort of by-blow from a failed affair, I didn't know. And, really, it was too much for me to ask about it. I was only an assistant hired to follow orders and keep my mouth shut.

I didn't realize Cyrille and I had both fallen silent—me because I was lost in thought and barely focused on my task, and he because he was lost in drawing me looking rather confused.

"She's watching us from one of the upper-floor windows," Cyrille suddenly said in a low voice. He kept drawing, his eyes moving rapidly from me to his sketchbook and back.

"Rowena?"

"Mrs. Quigg this time. No, don't look. She shouldn't know you're aware."

"But—why on earth is she doing this? Like Rowena—why?"

"Oh, heaven knows what goes on inside her head. No—I stand corrected. Only one thing goes on in her head, I'm afraid, and it's her mistress."

"I—I suppose I can see that. She's dreadfully fond and protective of Rowena."

"Mrs. Quigg never hides it, I know. But Mrs. Fairclough's easy enough to read. She covets you—as a companion. A son she never had, I suspect. A beautiful addition to her art. Perhaps Mrs. Quigg's attention has more to do with her seeing for herself that you're truly worthy of Mrs. Fairclough's maternal turns. In a way, she's her mistress's gatekeeper—the one whose good opinion everyone needs to earn in order to be allowed in Mrs. Fairclough's presence. Don't you agree?"

I stared at him with a grimace. "You're coming up with wild, fanciful stuff again. Just like an artist."

"Oh? You doubt me? Very well." Cyrille suddenly stopped his drawing, shut his sketchbook, and stumbled to his feet. "Come with me, darling."

He held out a hand, which I stared at for a second before taking in mine, and before I knew it, he was leading me into the trees. My basket sat abandoned amid the flowers and grass, and I found I really didn't care. I followed him as though I were in a trance, his grip firm and warm as he brought me deeper among the trees with sure steps.

Before long he stopped and then pulled something out of his pocket. It was a neatly tied bundle of discolored paper, and he pressed it into my hand and secured it there. Looking straight into my eyes, he said, "I need you to read these, Edgar. I know you have questions about my connection to Bridewater House—among other things. I—do know more about the lost child wandering the halls of Rowena's castle. Too much, in fact."

"What are these?"

"Letters—confession letters my grandfather wrote to my father. I bring them with me when I'm staying here for an extended time. My mother saved all of them, thinking they were enough to keep me from accepting Mrs. Fairclough's commissions. She called them a curse—one that killed my grandfather and then my father after."

I stared in horror at him. "Surely you don't mean you're on your way to being another victim!"

Cyrille chuckled. His earlier gravity eased into an affectionate sort of pleasure—at least I thought so, anyway, judging from the way he regarded me with that tender smile of his.

"I thought I was—for a time, I believed it. And then you came along." He kissed my forehead. "But please read them. And if you believe even partly in fairy tales, perhaps you're just the kind of prince I need to rescue me from a similar fate. No—we both are, aren't we? Two princes rescuing each other from someone's hungry shadow."

Chapter 18

Rowena's dining-room certainly burst with vibrant yellow and pink flowers that evening. Dinner was a "full table" so to speak, but despite the energetic conversation happening between Rowena and Cyrille, I found myself distracted and lost in thought from start to finish.

Not that it mattered, anyway. Rowena seemed determined to keep Cyrille's attention to herself, and I didn't care one bit. Cyrille's occasional glances at me reassured me his attention might be forced in one direction, but he was still very much aware of my presence there. I also thought I sensed an undercurrent of tenseness in him, a barely suppressed repugnance directed at the lady herself.

Whatever carefully woven façade he'd put on and kept on for months was quite likely unraveling before me. And I suspected, dismayed, that I was at fault somehow.

Ah! Ah!

A soft and too-familiar rattling reached my ears, the softness of the sound overriding the louder exchange from across the table as recognition drew me away from my companions. That whisper, too...

A tiny sound of surprise escaped me when I felt something nudge my foot, and I glanced down to find the ball roll to a stop beside my chair after gently striking my shoe. I stared at it for a horrified second or two, unable to form words, while the air around my chair turned icy.

Oh, God, I thought, my skin prickling. The ghost was there—somewhere beside me.

Then, just as suddenly, the chill faded, and warmth returned, but the ball taunted me with its unearthly presence. What on earth was I supposed to do with it now? Rowena and Cyrille appeared not to notice my blanched complexion and terror-filled gaze as I looked down at the ball again.

The child was trying to reach out to me again, I told myself. Oh, the poor lamb. I remembered Cyrille's own description of sensing the child watching from the shadows. It could only mean the unfortunate boy didn't find Cyrille worth the trouble to communicate with but felt comfortable enough with me.

Most likely because I was a stranger with a more tenuous connection to the house and its mistress.

I took a few calming breaths and eventually composed myself, waiting for the right moment when Rowena directed Cyrille's attention to a painting across the room and left me momentarily ignored. I immediately reached down and plucked the ball from the floor. It was small enough for me to stuff inside my jacket pocket, but I also needed to keep my hand there to hide its presence all the same. I stood up and excused myself from the table.

"Good night, my dear," Rowena said with a faint smile. "Pray remember the post tomorrow."

I spared Cyrille a glance and saw he'd ducked his head to avoid looking at me. "Yes, I'll remember. Good night."

My flight back to my room was barely memorable given the wild state of my mind then. The ball seemed to grow heavier and heavier with every step down the silent and dimly lit passageway. And when I finally reached my bedroom, I was quite breathless from my exertions though managed to remember to lock the door behind me. Not that it would have mattered to ghosts haunting the house, but the mere act certainly offered me some bit of comfort.

Mrs. Quigg had replaced my candelabrum with two more candle lamps and left a bundle of new candles and a box of matches near my bed. Three of those candle lamps might not be enough lighting to soothe my uneasiness toward the dark and what awaited me when the last flame was blown out, but I was too intent upon my purpose for retiring so soon to think much upon it. All the same, I was grateful for the cloudless sky outside and the unimpeded light offered by the moon.

After washing and changing to my nightshirt, I pulled out the bundle of letters Cyrille gave me earlier and settled myself on the bedcovers, sitting down and crossing my legs while gingerly setting one of the candle lamps close. At least the mattress was firm enough to keep it from teetering dangerously though I could hear my father's dismayed cries in my head.

In another moment, I was reading.

Everything was written in French, of course, but I understood it all. Indeed, by the end of it, I was heartily wishing I never learned the language in school.

The letter was really several brief messages written in sequence—like a journal, I thought. And it was, to my shock, a confession written by Cyrille's grandfather to the son. And just like that, everything I needed to know about the ghost, the Boivin family, Rowena Fairclough, and Bridewater House was largely explained.

Cyrille's grandfather was Modeste Boivin. He crossed paths with Rowena when she was quite young, and he was already long established in the art world as a painter of remarkable skill and promise. He also dabbled in sculpture but was mostly comfortable with paint and the brush.

He didn't say where they met exactly other than a "grand party" of some note. Rowena then was—I guessed—barely twenty but was already displaying qualities of a decisive and headstrong young woman. One, it also appeared, who was so bold as to be dangerously reckless.

But as it always happened, wealth took great care of her, and her wishes were granted, her orders followed, her desires satisfied—all without a word dared spoken in complaint, defiance, or correction. Modeste also described her as irresistibly charming and delightful, which may have made her path even smoother and more manageable given her sex and the limitations often saddling ladies like her.

She'd inherited a decrepit old property in a remote part of the country, but apparently she didn't care one bit about the isolation. She'd already dreamt of her castle and had spent countless hours improving upon her plan to rebuild the great house from the ground up.

"She was (and still is, I'm afraid) a creature fully invested in all things fanciful and fantastical," Modeste wrote. "And she believed wholeheartedly in crude superstition and old wives' tales despite her education and exquisite breeding. Perhaps it was boredom in one so young and so impossibly privileged. Or perhaps it was nothing more than a harmless turn so common among the young and naïve. But in Rowena Fairclough's hands, what would usually be darkly fanciful would take on a terrible life of its own."

Following some time spent in legal wrangling and other things involved in establishing full ownership of inherited property, reconstruction began in earnest.

"She requested the old studio to remain intact," the letter continued. It certainly confirmed what Mrs. Quigg had said about the room being the oldest part of the house. "But before any construction was done around it, she'd decided to ensure her castle's protection from harm—turning to superstition of the deadliest kind for what she needed."

It took me a few repeated efforts to go back and reread what came after given the chill that swept up and down my back at the scenes described. I was stunned into muteness for a moment, my brows creasing deeply as I struggled to comprehend the horror of having Rowena's new house protected.

A starving, desperate young mother had been convinced to sell her only—and equally unhealthy—child of four to Rowena. All was done in secret, of course, with the mother threatened with made-up crimes should she dare speak of it to anyone. Clearly she didn't and simply vanished from the rest of the story.

The little boy was described as having one foot in the grave already given his lack of food and proper care.

"The unfortunate creature wouldn't be missed by anyone," Modeste wrote. "Such was—and is—the case with these poor, starving wretches."

And so the boy was given an overdose of a sleeping draught, bundled up in what would be his burial shroud, and entombed while barely alive under the floor of the studio. With him were also buried a toy soldier and a toy ball, both of which he'd brought with him. He'd become the child sacrifice, Modeste said, that had been secretly practiced by some of the wealthy through the centuries. A barbaric superstition that drew on a person's darkest and basest instinct for the privilege of longevity, protection, perhaps even immortality in some form or other.

I choked out a sound of disgust and clamped a hand against my mouth though I knew no one else would hear me. I kept reading, horror, fury, and speechless revulsion threatening to make me vomit my dinner. Disbelief and grief turned into a spinning storm in my skull, and for the next moment, I passionately wished nothing but harm on everyone involved in the poor child's murder.

Yes, I wished the worst even on Cyrille's grandfather, who expressed extreme remorse for being a part of the whole thing—largely because he was apparently in love with Rowena but couldn't court her given their disparate worlds and ages.

Bridewater House gradually formed around the cursed studio, and Rowena showed her triumph over time and the real world by filling it immediately with all things fantastical. Art, impractical but very valuable furnishings and decorations, books, dinnerware and silver—she seemed to have thrown everything she could get her hands on into the house, stuffing it completely before turning her attention to the surrounding property.

The flower field was designed and fully executed to her specifications, the wood fencing the property carefully shaped with the felling of certain trees, and the temple erected in the clearing behind the house. By the time Rowena turned thirty, Bridewater House was perfected, and she laid claim to it as a proper mistress would.

"My crime will follow me to the grave, and it will haunt me well beyond. I have been one of the schemers. I was a thoughtless enabler of a woman whose beauty, charm, and endless store of money have stunted my judgment and twisted my nature. And an innocent child now lies dead and forgotten.

God help me, I don't even know the boy's name. No one does. Not Di Pasqua, not Schuyler. Rowena never even bothered to learn it, but I suspect she dared not for fear of having her conscience pricked and her resolve to get what she desired the most compromised by guilt."

I gave a start. Mr. Di Pasqua and Mr. Schuyler were two gentlemen to whom I'd written dictated letters. Both gentlemen, Cyrille also told me, were already dead. So they were also a part of the house's terrible history and not only because of their commissioned work. And perhaps that American gentleman I'd written to was also long dead though he wasn't mentioned here.

"Now and then I think I see the boy when I visit the lady. I think I hear his soft footfalls, his labored breathing because of his weakened lungs. Now and then I glimpse a shadow hovering just outside my line of sight, and when I turn, it's not there. I think he watches me from the shadows, perhaps wondering what I'm up to unless he's haunting my steps and accusing me (rightly) for my part in his murder. God help me! God help me!"

I'd reached the end of the confession now, and I could barely contain my tears. I turned my attention away from the horrors I'd just read to weep for the unhappy child. His movements, his insistence at getting my attention—all those made so much sense now. Above all, the loneliness and meek efforts at physical connection broke my heart and tore more wracking sobs from me.

"I will die cursed, and I will welcome whatever punishment's due me," Modeste continued. "I hope, my dear Eugène, you'll find it in your heart to forgive your wretched father. If you wish, keep this confession and give it to your son. He deserves to know what kind of a man his grandfather was. How an impossible amount of money promised by a beautiful woman butchered all reason and his moral compass.

"I must warn you, son, she will turn to you with more promises of wealth and success, and I hope—fervently and deeply—that you'd know better than to accede to any tempting offers she'd make. Despite my sins, I'd like to think I've raised you to be far superior to your accursed father. Rowena Fairclough has a touch of madness about her, and this child's murder will surely eat away at her mind. Indeed, her deterioration's already begun, I think. I've noticed things, and I've a feeling they'll only get worse.

"Be careful, Eugène. I beg of you. I won't be around for much longer, I know, because while Rowena's quite likely being driven out of her mind by her past, I'm falling ill from a wrecked conscience. I desire peace though I know I'll never have it even in death. And absolution? I dare not hope for any. I'm leaving for the last time for Bridewater House. There I'll remain until the child calls for me one last time, and I'll gladly, wearily follow."

A short note followed the last paragraph, and it was written in a different hand.

"The child called on the 7th of July, 18— , and Papa answered. May God have mercy on his soul."

No other information was written as to how Modeste Boivin died, but did it matter in the end?

As for Eugène, I could only wonder why he carried on the connection with Rowena. Perhaps money was involved because he was quite likely married by then and raising a family. He needed money, and as a young artist, accepting commissions from his father's patron must have been an easy solution to his dilemma. I couldn't blame him at all if his circumstances were dire, but I also couldn't say the same for Cyrille. I suspect his reference to a debt must have been to the poor, nameless boy.

Chapter 19

I didn't feel well when I rose the following morning. Given the ghastly time I had last night, I couldn't make myself get up and be useful. I felt too wrung out, my eyes still swollen, my nose stuffed up, and—this was the worst bit—I simply knew too much now. And I didn't have the mental fortitude to present myself to Rowena or even Cyrille that day, so I made my excuse when one of the maids quietly knocked on my door to remind me of the final half hour of breakfast.

It was nearly a month since I first entered Bridewater House. I'd yet to visit my father, and I'd yet to hear back from him. Personally, I didn't feel as though I'd improved myself or done anything significant. I just existed, caught in a never-ending breeze the way a dead leaf would tumble and roll and skitter, propelled forward over the ground with no direction or purpose.

Time seemed to move so differently here in that time didn't seem to exist at all. No matter where I looked, I was beset by reminders of things that didn't belong in the present world. Artwork, furnishings, decorative touches—I felt like one of those hapless insects trapped in amber. Caught in perpetual suspension, any process of further decay completely stopped.

I was made to pose and dress a certain way, manipulated like a child's doll at playtime. I was no better than a puppet on strings, moved by a puppeteer whose aim remained unspoken though it was clearly laid out in her head from the way her eyes lit up when she watched me. I was made to write business letters to people who'd died a long time ago.

Madness, yes—I was being generously paid to be a part of a madwoman's phantasmagorical world. I thought of the unfortunate boy lying forgotten somewhere under the canvases and paint spills and rags. How grotesquely fitting it was for his resting-place to be the focal point of everything unreal and yet not in Rowena's world.

I groaned and rubbed my temples when another wave of pain assaulted my poor head. I should eat something, but I still didn't want to show myself downstairs.

Indeed, all I wanted then was to demand my pay and then tender my resignation, my bags in hand. Being a part of Rowena's dark fantasy made me ill, and the longer I pondered (however painfully), the more firmly I resolved to leave no later than a month, which was the agreed-upon time allowed me to test the waters as Rowena's new employee.

I suppose I could manage a month's wages. I should be able to make the money stretch for as long as I could while I looked for other work. Poor Papa. How disappointed he'd be though I was sure he'd be reassuring and supportive of my choice.

"There," I muttered at my haggard reflection, the water I'd just splashed on my face dripping down and making me look even more wrecked. "I've decided. I'll leave in..." I paused and calculated my time there. "I'll leave in a week. Five days, actually."

I took a deep breath, bent down again, and splashed more water to clear my aching head further. When I stood straight, I reached for a towel and dried my face, and when I opened my eyes, I saw him in the mirror, looking blankly at me as he stood just behind. A small, sickly-looking thing in rags.

"Oh, God!" I cried as I spun around and stumbled, caught my foot on the rug, and fell on the floor.

The boy wasn't there, of course. He was nowhere to be seen other than that one brief glimpse in the mirror. I felt the warmth of the bright morning sun blanket me, embrace me with golden comfort. Frantic glances around the room revealed nothing else—no one else—and I was truly alone. Breathing in ragged bursts, I scrambled to my feet and hobbled to my bed, where I collapsed and fought to gather my wits.

I didn't know how long it took for me to calm down at last, but I eventually did. Dressing up after that horrific scare seemed like a moment spent in a fogged trance then I was walking down the passageway, the ball in hand.

Nothing but silence met me as I half-staggered along. I hoped no one was in the studio that morning because I needed to be there alone. An urgent need to present myself to the dead and offer—what, really? Comfort? How could one comfort a murdered child? His search for his mother would never end. I could see that now. Yet a compulsion as fierce and powerful as I'd never felt before spurred me on and directed my steps despite my confusion and doubts as to what I should do next. I only had the ball for guidance for all the good that gave me.

When I reached the top landing, I heard muffled voices raised in anger down the passageway leading to Rowena's and Cyrille's bedrooms. I couldn't make out whose voices they were, but it didn't hinder me at all. I simply had to go to the studio *now*.

I saw none of the servants along the way, but I did catch distant conversations that spoke of mundane tasks and normal domestic scenes elsewhere. There was nothing mundane or normal where I was headed, and when I turned the final corner leading to the rear of the house and the studio, I stumbled to a halt at the sight of the studio's closed door slowly opening. It didn't creak at all though I knew it should. It moved as an ancient door on barely maintained hinges would unless propelled by an unseen child with hardly any strength left.

"I'm here," I whispered. "I have your toy."

I walked slowly toward the now gaping door, shivering at the threshold when a wall of cold air struck me. Despite the sunlight filtering through the windows and the rear door that had been thrown wide open to welcome the outside air, a sepulchral hollowness permeated the air in the studio.

I walked inside, unsure where to go. The body could be anywhere, I thought as I scanned the littered floor.

"Where are you, my dear?" I asked.

I paused somewhere near the giant easel in the middle of the room. The canvas sitting on it was quite done, I noticed as I stepped closer for a more thorough inspection. The painting was that of Rowena dressed in an idealized peasant girl's costume—the shepherdess costume. She stood under the shadow of a tree and cradled a swaddled infant in her arms. But her attention wasn't on the baby she held but on another figure standing nearby and in the sun.

The figure was tall and pale, its features barely seen because of the layers of tattered white cloth wrapped around its entire figure. It leaned unnervingly close, clearly intent upon the little baby though it didn't touch the child—merely bent precariously close to it, its face just a few inches away from the baby's. The figure made my hair stand on end. Despite its lack of detailed features—or perhaps partly because of it—the shrouded figure impressed upon me the most awful feeling of dread and horror. That its wrapped form echoed the baby's, in fact, though the baby's face still showed in a state of peaceful slumber.

Rowena, on the other hand, clutched the child against her chest in an attitude of desperate protection, her beautiful features contorted in a mask of mute terror as she stared at the shrouded figure. Her baby was about to be taken away,

I thought, my heart pounding as the scene unfolded further in my head. Rowena leaned away from the bent figure, which ignored her completely as if Rowena didn't exist or mattered in the slightest, though she also seemed to be rooted to the spot where she stood. If she sought protection in the tree's shadow, she wasn't getting any.

Her surroundings were no different from the bucolic settings I'd grown so used to seeing being proudly displayed in those magnificent and ostentatious frames. But the dreadful tableau in the center of the painting revealed a darker story—one I was sure Rowena wouldn't have stood for.

Breathless and wide-eyed, I scanned the painting until I saw words irregularly scraped into the thick paint near the bottom of the canvas: *Et in Arcadia Ego*.

"Cyrille," I breathed, dismayed. "What on earth have you done?"

A slight noise from elsewhere in the studio drew my attention to the canvases leaning against the wall. I hurried over and went through each, seeing that they were all half-finished or nearly finished paintings of Rowena in the sort of perfect fairy tale setting she'd always preferred.

I'd seen them before, of course, but I never really gave them much thought. Before now, I saw them as failed attempts or perhaps even practice pieces meant to be painted over or even improved upon when the time was right, and Cyrille once again felt inspired enough to complete it.

But that had all been before this awful revelation of the house's history and the terrible role Rowena had played in its construction. Were these unfinished canvases then a sign of Cyrille's revulsion toward Bridewater House and everything it contained? A show of disgust toward his patron, knowing what his grandfather had taken part in?

So what was the reason for his taking on the commissions then? From what I was told, all of the paintings and sculptures in the house were done by Modeste and Eugène and his twin while Cyrille had yet to complete something. If he was so reluctant, why take on her offer? The money? Rowena was extremely generous in her compensation, to be sure, but I knew Cyrille wouldn't be so easily swayed with him so young with no wife or child to feed and clothe if he detested her so much.

I turned toward the painting on the easel again, my mind racing as I struggled to piece so many things together.

Et in Arcadia Ego.

Even in Arcadia, there am I.

My breath left me as realization dawned. "Oh, Cyrille," I whispered. "Why?"

It was stupid question, in truth. Of course I knew why he refused to finish any of the "proper" paintings and, quite likely, worked hard on the displayed one behind Rowena's back. It was justice for the dead child. Perhaps with a touch of vengeance, even.

By refusing to complete Rowena's commissions so pointedly—even dragging things out with conversations and endless hours spent in the studio going over Rowena's schemes for her new collection—he'd done what his father and grandfather couldn't. He'd stood firm and denied the dangerous fantasies of a woman in the grip of spiraling madness in spite of the promised wealth.

He'd kept his grandfather's confession close to him for God knew how long now, a reminder of a crime done so many years ago and the blood that had stained his kin's hands.

Cyrille had been rather cavalier about things when we spoke about the ghost and barely showed his deeper emotions when he gave me the confessions. Indeed, there was a certain ruthlessness to the way he managed to control himself, and when I thought of those fleeting moments in Rowena's company where I noticed a certain hardness in her gaze...

I knew she'd met her match in Cyrille Boivin. And judging from the ghoulish painting he'd proudly set on his easel for all the world to see, it was clear he knew exactly what he was doing and what he wanted from all this.

Without speaking a word, he'd accused Rowena of the crime of murder. He'd forced death into a fairy tale. He'd wished her to see and be reminded of—be haunted by—her past and the nameless innocent who'd paid the ultimate price for her vanity.

And would this aggressive exposure drive Rowena's guilt-burdened mind so far beyond help? I could see no offer of forgiveness in the painting. Every exquisite and gentle brushstroke, every carefully rendered detail, every gentle opposition of light and shadow felt more like a mockery with Cyrille's fury and outrage hidden under such skill.

I didn't know how long I stood there, numbness slowly taking over the shock and horror that had me in their grip for a while. I even forgot I still held the little ball until I felt it gently tugged from my hand, and I looked down in time to see it knocked out of my grip and roll away.

It rolled for several inches and then came to a sudden stop on a part of the floor between the easel and the rear door.

There I am.

Et in Arcadia Ego.

I understood then and numbly, tearfully, searched for a pointed or sharp tool. I found some sort of pointed instrument—an awl—and went to the ball, pushing away all detritus until I cleared a small patch of the stone floor. I then scratched a cross where the ball sat, pressing hard on the awl and going over the lines several times until a dark enough symbol could be seen despite its crudeness. I set my tool aside and sat back on my heels while pressing a hand over the cross.

One could say the studio's the heart of the house given what it contains.

"I'm very sorry," I whispered as tears spilled. "I'm so, so sorry this happened to you. I hope you find peace soon. I won't be staying long here, I'm afraid. I won't be able to keep you company anymore." I dashed away the tears and composed myself with some effort. "I'll never forget you though I don't know your name."

Cynical minds might sniff and say that I didn't mean it—that I'd forget as soon as I left Bridewater House forever. But I didn't. I don't think I ever would.

Chapter 20

I was summoned to the temple for an unexpected reading time by a grim-faced Mrs. Quigg. She appeared distracted and in a foul mood, and I wondered if she was one of the voices I'd heard earlier as I hastened down to the studio.

I appeared at the quaint little folly with the Ann Radcliffe book I'd been trying to read to Rowena and found her sitting stiff and straight like a queen, her gaze intense and wide as she stared at something in the trees. She didn't even seem to realize I was there despite the sound of my movements and my quiet greeting.

"I have yet to pay you," she said after a moment's awkward silence. She never looked at me as she spoke. "You were never compensated—at least not yet."

"No, ma'am," I replied. I didn't catch myself or correct my use of "ma'am" that time. I saw no point. I couldn't look at her the same way as before. "I—I believe the contract said one month, which is the end of my trial period."

A trial month I no longer wished to complete. I then wondered if this was the sort of thing the girls before me experienced as well, but at the same time, something also told me this—that is, my experiences—were vastly different from theirs.

Cyrille had said they didn't feel at ease in the house, but then again, I also understood he hadn't been working for Rowena for too long. A mere six months, I think, while his grandfather lasted several years and Cyrille's father, even longer than that. With everything I now knew, I wouldn't be surprised if Cyrille never intended to stay and perhaps gave himself a set length of time to do what he felt he needed and then remove himself from this cursed place forever. He'd blithely said my presence had hastened things for him, and I thought I understood now.

"You won't need to wait that long, Mr. Cushing."

"Thank you, ma'am."

Rowena turned her attention to me, and the odd and barely seen hardness in her gaze was there.

"I need you to sit over there—outside the shelter of the temple, on the grass. I want just the right amount of sunlight touching you so you look something like an otherworldly beauty. Maybe even a young scholar from the land of fairy. Take your jacket off and tousle your hair just so. And—undo your cravat a little. I want a certain carelessness in your appearance today when you read to me."

I glanced at the spot where she'd indicated and held the book close. It didn't take long for me to find my voice again, let alone my courage. My mind drifted back to that cross I'd carved into the stone floor in the studio, and my heart hardened, echoing the ice-blue coldness in Rowena's eyes.

"I'm afraid I can't," I said. "I'm—I'm tendering my resignation, Mrs. Fairclough. I can't carry on working for you in this capacity."

"I see."

She fell silent and observed me with that awful gaze. Her dress, fashionable and richly made, looked incongruent on her. Though it had only been less than a day since we were in each other's company, she seemed to have wilted further. Her complexion had taken on an ashen and yet somewhat translucent hue, her skin seeming to have lost all bulk and so now hugged her bones with nothing to give it form. Her pale eyes were even more deeply shadowed, her hair even airier and looking more like a halo of strands that had belonged to someone else and simply transferred to her.

"Nothing feels like a greater betrayal than a refusal of one's dearest wish from one's own son."

I blinked. "What? Son? What son?"

"Tell me, my dear, since you're so intent upon leaving me—as children as expected to do someday, I suppose—will you refuse me one last thing?"

I didn't know what to think now, my confusion surely showing itself quite clearly on my face. I frowned though I felt far more dread than irritation, and somehow I managed to blurt out, "What one last thing, ma'am?"

Rowena appeared to consider what to do next and then gave a sharp nod. "Come here."

I had no choice but to obey, and before long I stood before her, the book still held close like a shield. Another moment of terrible silence unfolded before Rowena raised a hand and rested it against the side of my face—a tender, loving, wondering touch.

"What a waste of youth, innocence, and beauty," she murmured, gently stroking her palm across my skin. "We'd have made a marvelous pair in Boivin's art. Leto and her shining Apollo. Maia and her winged Hermes. Penelope and her noble Telemachus. Bridewater House would have burned brighter on its foundations if I had my way—mother and son together. Immortal and untouchable. Parthenogenesis in its most glorious."

She sighed then though her gaunt face stayed unreadable and marble-like. She gave my cheek another tender stroke before she pulled her hand away, swung hard, and struck me across the face. My head snapped to the right, and I staggered back and dropped the book, nearly losing my balance from such an unexpected and vicious assault.

"Go then, my dear. Rest assured you'll be paid handsomely for your valiant efforts at entertaining a mad old spinster. Our supplies will be coming by in an hour, and you may get on the cart and have the driver take you wherever you need to go. Goodbye."

I stood in speechless shock, my hand cradling my throbbing cheek. I just blinked stupidly and then retrieved the book, which she ordered I leave with her, and then went back inside. My walk back to my room was all a dream-like blur with so many events happening far too rapidly for me to keep up. I couldn't even remember any real break or uneventful moment when I was allowed some respite from Rowena's grotesque world.

I spotted a note lying on my pillow, and I saw it was from Cyrille.

"Do what you will to my grandfather's confessions, my darling, as I've done what I needed to and am ready to move on. I'm no longer employed by the fair Rowena Fairclough and leave the premises uncompensated as punishment, but I promise you this isn't the last you'll hear from me. I shall write you again soon enough as I have my methods of discovering little secrets when I set my mind to it. Like your address, for instance. Think of me bold and reckless, but I'm not quite done courting you, my sweet Edgar. I'll be rather busy looking for work for a time, so my re-entry as a proper suitor won't be for a little while," he said.

I could imagine that roguish little smile on his face when he wrote this letter, and while I regretted his methods of ensuring justice for that poor child, I knew I also wouldn't have been able to do anything for the boy, either. Perhaps it was a lack of imagination or cunning on my part, but one also needed to consider the dreadful connection Cyrille had with Rowena and that, in his mind, it needed to be severed with such a brutal force as to ensure its finality.

Perhaps it was guilt also eating relentlessly away at his heart and conscience, knowing full well what his grandfather had done—for love and for money. As for Cyrille's father? I'd yet to learn more, but it could wait. What was done was done, and there was simply no way for anyone to change the past. Cyrille couldn't forgive, and I thought I understood.

Along with the note, Cyrille left me an entire sketchbook filled with more watercolor studies of me. He certainly wasn't joking when he said he'd kept himself busy while away from Bridewater House for a few days. I couldn't help the indulgent little chuckle escaping me, and I pressed a fond kiss onto the book's cover before gathering the rest of my darling's gifts and bundling them with the sketchbook.

Before long I was completely packed and ready to go with ten minutes to spare before the cart of supplies rumbled down the drive. I took Modeste's confessions and walked one final time toward Rowena's study. I met no one there, thankfully, and when I entered the empty study, I hurried to the desk. Ignoring the memory of time spent scribbling letter after letter to long-dead artists and craftsmen on that imposing piece of furniture, I unfolded the confessions, flattened out the discolored sheets as well as I could, and arranged them all on the desk directly before the chair.

I didn't care who'd find them—Mrs. Quigg first, most likely—because everything contained in those sheets of paper belonged solely to the past and the rotten core of Bridewater House. It wouldn't have mattered if the housekeeper came upon it, anyway. She knew about the child—of that I was quite sure now. She'd burned the toy soldier, completely erasing one essential part of the child's existence, and that told me she'd done so to protect her mistress.

"I'm done here," I muttered, shaking my head as another familiar wave of disgust swept through me, this time in response to Mrs. Quigg and her false friendliness and openness.

She was just as guilty as the others in aiding and abetting Rowena's terrible fantasies. It would also be pointless for me to reach out to authorities over a murder decades-old. Justice, I thought, was working quietly, steadily, in the background all these years, forcing Rowena and Mrs. Quigg inexorably down a path worse than the noose.

It wasn't long before I was being helped into the dirt-caked cart, my bags properly stowed in the back, my jacket pocket stuffed with my pay. I still couldn't believe the amount that was given me. I suppose in that sense I did respect Rowena Fairclough for being true to her word. Even Mrs. Quigg, who'd handed me the envelope with a look of mild contempt and without a word uttered as I struggled with my bags out the front doors, honored her mistress's command.

The driver ignored my protests and turned his cart down the opposite direction just to take me back to Bracklewhyte. I'd been ready to look for another pony and trap for hire wherever he was headed, but he'd insisted, claiming he didn't have much else to do now that he'd taken care of Mrs. Fairclough's supplies for the week.

My ride home was very pleasant and freeing. I suppose it helped greatly that my companion knew nothing of the terrifying secrets of the great house he'd just left, and we both carried on with our conversation with no real purpose other than to lighten the tiresome journey over the rough, gravelly road. Before long we were laughing at each other's stories and jokes though he certainly knew a great deal more than I did when it came to the absurdities of human nature.

Neither Bernard nor Mrs. Murray was at home when I reached it, but I could have dropped to my face and kissed the ground before my father's modest little house and danced and capered for a time.

"Papa?" I whispered upon entering his room and finding him sitting up and reading.

He turned and hissed a shocked breath. "Edgar? Is that you, son?"

I hurried to him, arms wide open, and all but collapsed in tearful joy in his arms as he held me tightly, laughing and talking and full of wonder and questions. He waited for me to calm down, stroking my hair gently and pulling away to pepper my face with kisses.

"My boy, my precious boy," he said again and again in a voice that broke though tears didn't flow.

Bernard had gone off on an errand but was expected back soon. Mrs. Murray had also gone home but was set to return for dinner. Between lunch and tea, we were quite stuck with whatever Bernard would manage to put together in the kitchen, but I didn't care. I'd sooner have a loaf of stale bread and cold tea over the most perfectly cooked array of meat and vegetables that had been my reality for the last few weeks.

What madness was it, I thought, that I'd only been away for a little less than a month, and yet it felt as though I'd been out on the longest and most exhausting journey imaginable.

I told Papa everything while we waited for Bernard to return. I might have waited till the proper time to unload such things on him, but with my sudden and startling return home, I simply had no excuse. Papa listened with growing concern and horror, and his hold on my hands tightened. Then I showed him my one and only pay, which tore a squawk of surprise from him.

"Good lord," he breathed. "It's one thing for me to hear about the amount. It's another to actually see it laid out on paper."

"Mrs. Fairclough at least honored her end of the bargain," I replied, regret lacing through my words as I looked at my wages. "I think she's just too proud to do anything but."

"I think you're right, my boy." Papa ruffled my hair playfully. "What do you intend to do now?"

"Rest for a day and go out and look for another job, of course. Come now, Papa. You know this won't last us if I just sat around and got too comfortable. Besides, you're supposed to help me this time. I don't want to answer another help wanted post and end up in another haunted house with a terrible history."

"No, indeed. Can't have that again, can we?" Papa said with a bark of laughter.

The rest of the day—over lunch first and then over tea and then dinner—I pored over more help wanted ads. This time I had not only Papa on hand to help me decide which posts sounded legitimate and which ones sounded too good to be true, but also Bernard and—after an excruciating moment being embraced and kissed within an inch of my life while she wept loudly with joy—Mrs. Murray.

By the time I retired, I had several good prospects to pursue. In another week, I was employed once again as an assistant at a stationer's shop, my new workplace just a few minutes' walk from my home. The pay was dreadfully poor comparatively, but as I watched my perpetually baffled, kind-hearted, and soft-spoken employer look for a hand-bound journal he'd apparently misplaced, I thought I'd never felt so rich in my life.

Chapter 21

Cyrille made good his word, appearing from nowhere and surprising me at the shop close to a year after I left Bridewater House. He'd secured work—commissions, of course, for a mix of art patrons and a couple of ambitious entrepreneurs who wished to turn Cyrille's miniatures into collectibles for wealthy fanciers of unique ephemera. Whatever that might mean, I hasten to add.

Before that, he proved himself a most determined and faithful suitor. Throughout the year he'd send me letters apprising me of his activities and whereabouts, which he'd always end with declarations of love and sweet promises of coming home to me once he established himself. Of that I was never in any doubt, and I responded accordingly.

The shop had just closed for the day, and Mr. Beyersdorf, my employer, had shuffled off to the back room to work on the books. The old gentleman might be a bit absent-minded when it came to the movements of his inventory on the floor, but he showed a remarkably sharp mind where it mattered the most (in his opinion, anyway), and that was the books and that day's sales.

I'd just finished sweeping the floor when I heard soft knocks on the locked door. I glanced up, a tired retort on my lips, when I recognized the brightly grinning face peering into the window.

"Cyrille?" I whispered after a moment's shocked silence. "Cyrille!"

With a little cry of delight, I dropped my broom and all but leapt to the door, unlocking it and throwing it open in order to pull Cyrille inside and throwing my arms around him. I felt his wrap around my waist with a tightness I'd always dreamt of as he lifted me off the floor with a burst of laughter. We held each other thus for a minute or so, alternately laughing and stammering exclamations of disbelief.

"Mr. Cushing? Is there someone out there with you?" Mr. Beyersdorf called from the depths of the shop. The back room was situated behind the main shop, fully separated by the wall behind the counter, its single door only slightly open.

"A good friend of mine, sir! He's just come back from his travels!" I called back without loosening my hold on my darling Cyrille. He let me slide down to the floor, both of us beaming at each other all the while.

"Splendid news then," Mr. Beyersdorf exclaimed. He never bothered to stand up during conversations like this, complaining of his aching joints and tired muscles. Staying seated behind his desk while shouting through the partly open door was apparently far preferable to the poor old gentleman. "Have you finished with the sweeping?"

"Yes, sir!"

"Very well, then. Go on and enjoy the rest of the evening with your friend. I'll see you tomorrow morning."

"Thank you, Mr. Beyersdorf! Thank you!"

I hurried off with the broom, which I returned to its little closet before undoing my smock and shrugging on my jacket. In another moment Cyrille and I were walking slowly down the street, lost in conversation as the shadows of the early evening lengthened. He told me everything about his adventures in employment-seeking, most of which I'd already learned from his letters.

I also gave him a good summary of my own comings and goings since my return home. It really didn't take me long since I never moved around beyond work, home, and the occasional errand when Bernard wasn't available. All in all my life after a month in Bridewater House had become awfully dull and mundane, but I'd rather have that any day.

I introduced Cyrille to Papa after and then to Mrs. Murray and Bernard. We all enjoyed a delightful dinner, with Cyrille charming my awestruck father with stories of his travels as he searched for patrons.

"I'd take you both to France with me someday, I hope," he said with a wink at me, and I couldn't hide a blush. I was just glad my father didn't notice it, his attention wholly fixed on our guest of honor. "There's so many quiet places you can go to rest and recuperate properly, monsieur. A few weeks lost somewhere in a village in the shadows of Mont Blanc would surely do you good."

Throughout the meal, I thought I noticed Papa glance between me and Cyrille with a curious and somewhat thoughtful air. I was very careful not to let on about my heart and Cyrille's full ownership of it, but parents always knew, didn't they? Papa likely suspected, but to his great credit, he raised no fuss afterward and only pulled me close for an embrace and a kiss on the cheek. All the years since, he'd never said a single word about my bachelorhood and my close friendship with Cyrille Boivin.

It was perhaps three years after—when I finally turned twenty-one—that news of the fate of Bridewater House and its mistress reached my ears.

I was summoned to a solicitor's office a great distance away, which necessitated a good deal of packing and a bit of planning for some time spent enjoying a respite from work. Cyrille was away then, having secured another commission from a collector who lived somewhere in Spain. And in that solicitor's office, I learned that I was made heir to all of Rowena's money and property. Her will, I understood, had been written a few years before our paths crossed, and it hadn't been revisited until recently—when she named me her heir.

In truth, I could barely recall much of the conversation, the solicitor's rambling explanations being so tightly wrapped up in legal language I couldn't even understand. It certainly didn't help that the shock of finding out about the extreme shift in my situation had rendered me not only speechless, but dizzy and nearly faint as well.

The long and short of it was that, yes, I would inherit Rowena's money and her property, including Bridewater House, the land, and everything it contained. Including, of course, its lost, lonely ghost.

"Why—what happened to Mrs. Fairclough?" I breathed once the gentleman paused in his rambling account.

"The lady passed on two years ago, Mr. Cushing, or you wouldn't be here," came the dry reply. "There was a good deal of wrangling over her will, and I was, unfortunately, also quite tied up with a few other matters involving other clients that I wasn't able to sort things out for her until a few months ago."

"How did she die?"

Illness, I was told. Rowena had simply faded and wasted away, her faculties slipping until she was nothing but a mere shell of her former self. Eventually she stopped eating and drinking altogether and died in bed. Her death was, sadly, expected given how long and gradual her fragile health deteriorated further.

"How awful," I murmured, shocked. "I—I hope she passed peacefully enough."

The solicitor snorted. "Hardly. You do know she'd become quite mad, yes? Well, you can only imagine how someone burdened with so many troubled fancies would spend their final hours. I wasn't there, of course, but people talk. And with the unfortunate lady, there was a good deal of talk going around if you believe any such nonsense."

There were accounts—unverified, apparently—of her calling out to someone whose name she never uttered.

"Where is he? Where's my poor boy? My son? Why has he left me alone? Such a beautiful boy but so cruel to his mother!" There were also rumors of her staring in wide-eyed horror at something no one else could see in different parts of her bedroom. "Who's that? Why does he keep troubling me? Tell him to go away!" Or something along those lines, I was told.

She was buried with due respect and solemn ceremony. Then the servants were all dismissed until Mrs. Quigg was all who was left to look after Bridewater House. The housekeeper, faithful to the end, had tended to her dying mistress, and I daresay she'd voiced a most fervent vow to look after Rowena's beloved house until she breathed her last.

Which Mrs. Quigg had done, the solicitor said with a look of dismay and regret.

"The housekeeper died in the house alone two months or so after her mistress," he said, lacing his fingers together on his desk. "She was discovered perhaps a fortnight later—when the alarm was raised after the fellow who brought her supplies had to turn back every week because she didn't open the door to him the way she used to."

I listened with growing horror. I imagined Mrs. Quigg, perhaps overcome by illness herself after grieving over her late mistress, carrying on with her duties day after excruciatingly lonely day. Her footsteps echoing loudly through the empty passageways and rooms of an isolated house. Hearing nothing but her own breathing, her own movements, and perhaps her occasional self-directed conversations. Unless she held one-sided conversations with Rowena as she went about her usual tasks, of course. Dear God, what an existence!

That said, I truly doubted if Mrs. Quigg minded at all. She would have said yes to everything Rowena did, no matter what it might be. To be sure, she'd encouraged and enabled Rowena's fantasies in the way a tragically misguided mother would demonstrate her blind devotion to her most beloved child.

I never really knew Mrs. Quigg—her story, her mind, her heart—I simply never got the chance, but many things happen for a reason, and I suppose this was one of those instances where I was meant to be left in the dark. Perhaps even spend the rest of my life speculating about this strange and terrible housekeeper.

Suffice it to say, I signed the papers thrust into my hands but decided not to claim Bridewater House. I allowed the structure to fall into ruin despite all of the wealth and magnificent contents it held within. I was still the master of Rowena's dilapidated fairy tale. I simply would never move into a house I now knew was cursed, and if the restless ghost of a murdered child roamed its shadowy hallways, what of its dead mistress and her fanatical hold on the physical structure and everything it represented? And what of the housekeeper who gladly welcomed the role of silent guardian and protector?

All three had a connection to the house itself, each of them somehow defined by its existence, their lives so tightly woven into the tapestry of Bridewater House's past that no amount of redecorating or reconstruction from its new master would sever these links. The darkest corners of the human heart stitched their lives inextricably together, and death made the bond permanent. Had I agreed to move my father into the great house, my hours would have been dogged by three ghosts.

No—I wouldn't chance it, not with my father in his ruined physical state.

And there I left things—I gratefully accepted Rowena's largesse, however misguided it might appear to others, though I barely touched the money other than to pay for Papa's medication and extra needs. He improved greatly over time but never found work again. It didn't matter to me. I took care of him by sticking to my job for a couple more years after.

Papa and Cyrille were quite shocked upon hearing of my sudden turn of fortune and, indeed, first expressed doubts. But when time passed and no challenge or suits were brought against Rowena's solicitor for improperly executing her will, stunned relief set in. Cyrille confessed to at first wishing I never touched the money, but seeing how much help my father needed, he agreed it was for the best.

It was my idea to pay midnight visits to Bridewater House on randomly chosen dates since hearing about Mrs. Quigg's death. I needed to see for myself—remind myself, that is—just how wisely I chose in not moving into Bridewater House. Perhaps I hovered dangerously close to developing my own obsession, but fortunately I had Cyrille anchoring me to reality.

Each of those midnight visits revealed to me just how tightly the dead kept their hold on their former world. Cyrille and I would stand in horrified awe as we watched Mrs. Quigg's candle lamp flicker in the thick darkness of the upper-floor windows. Room after room, so faint yet so terribly clear—she continued to wander the silent ruins, ensuring her beloved mistress's castle was kept to her exacting standards.

I imagined somewhere in the deepest, blackest spaces within, Rowena walked with faltering steps. From room to room, gazing at her unchanging likenesses in discolored and moldy canvas and paint, brushing past thickening cobwebs and dusty nymphs.

Perhaps walking alongside her, reaching up to clasp her cold hand for long-denied companionship and comfort, was the little boy whose death ultimately shaped Bridewater House's destiny as a rotting temple to vanity and immortality.

Once Cyrille, Papa, and I stepped foot in France, my nightmares vanished, and I gradually learned to stop looking back. I'm now twenty-four with a hopeful future ahead of me. I've found new, fulfilling work where I currently live, and I'm quite pleased. Leave the dead alone and leave them far, far behind. Where I'm headed, where I keep my eager gaze has no room for regrets or dreary shadows and tragedies.

I have my father, who perhaps understands me and my heart better than I've ever hoped though he still keeps his peace and has welcomed Cyrille with much affection as one would expect from any doting father-in-law.

I also have Cyrille, my beloved un-husband, in whose arms I find peace and contentment, in whose love I find the strength to undo every ghastly stitch Rowena Fairclough had managed to weave into my dreams and memories. My shining Apollo, my winged Hermes, my noble Telemachus.

Don't miss out!

Visit the website below and you can sign up to receive emails whenever Hayden Thorne publishes a new book. There's no charge and no obligation.

https://books2read.com/r/B-A-LFQC-HLMSB

About the Author

I've lived most of my life in the San Francisco Bay Area though I wasn't born there (or, indeed, the USA). I'm married with no kids and three cats.

I started off as a writer of gay young adult fiction, specializing in contemporary fantasy, historical fantasy, and historical genres. My books ranged from a superhero fantasy series to reworked and original folktales to Victorian ghost fiction.

I've since expanded to gay New Adult fiction, which reflects similar themes as my YA books and varies considerably in terms of romantic and sexual content.

While I've published with a small press in the past, I now self-publish my books. Please visit my site for exclusive sales and publishing updates.

Read more at https://www.haydenthorne.com.